machine

Also by Susan Steinberg

Spectacle
Hydroplane
The End of Free Love

machine

a novel

Susan Steinberg

Graywolf Press

Excerpts from this novel appeared originally in different form in the follow-
ing publications:
"Killers" in *American Short Fiction*
"Machines" in the *Believer*
"Saviors" in *ZYZZYVA*

This publication is made possible, in part, by the voters of Minnesota through
a Minnesota State Arts Board Operating Support grant, thanks to a legisla-
tive appropriation from the arts and cultural heritage fund. Significant support has also been provided by the National Endowment for the Arts, Target,
the McKnight Foundation, the Lannan Foundation, the Amazon Literary
Partnership, and other generous contributions from foundations, corpora-
tions, and individuals. To these organizations and individuals we offer our
heartfelt thanks.

Published by Graywolf Press
250 Third Avenue North, Suite 600
Minneapolis, Minnesota 55401

www.graywolfpress.org

Published in the United States of America

ISBN 978-1-55597-847-1

2 4 6 8 9 7 5 3 1
First Graywolf Printing, 2019

Library of Congress Control Number: 2018910930

Cover design: Kimberly Glyder

Cover art: Joe LoBianco / Getty Images

Contents

machine

Killers

the water is deeper than it looks; and we're not the worst swim-
mers, but it's dark; we tend not to swim at night; no, we tend
not to swim at night with guys; we all knew of the girl who
drowned; she sank like a stone, they said; she was showing off
that night, they said; the guys all said;

tonight, it's guys we meet at the boathouse; they're here for the
end of summer; they're beautiful in a polished way; but we're
beautiful in that polished way; we look out across the water;
we whisper nothing and pretend it's more; so the guys look
over or don't look over; either way, it means the same thing;

at some point, they'll be done with us; we'll have wasted their
time, they'll say; so they'll threaten us; they'll terrorize us; So

kill us, we'll say and laugh too hard like fuck these guys; like who the fuck are these guys;

this summer, we learn we're part of a demographic; we're girls who go to private schools; girls at the tops of our classes; girls who stay at the shore all summer and become the stars of the shore;

so this summer, we learn we're split into two; I learn we're split into more than two; I wouldn't say we're shattered; we're not in pieces across your floor; it's more, I would say, like fractured; I would say, like cracked;

the ride to the shore this summer was long, and no one talked; I lay across the back seat watching clouds; I slept and dreamed my parents were singing loudly in the front; but when I woke, my mother was sleeping, her head drooped to her chest; my father was staring straight ahead; the radio was playing the song from my dream; it wasn't the song I would have played, were I in charge; that song would have been good and loud; the windows would have been all the way down; my parents wouldn't have been there;

mornings, my father sits with me at the table; he's mad at me, he says; I've been coming home too late, he says; I've been coming home too drunk; but I can barely listen to my father; something is going on with him; I can't say, exactly, what it is; so I'll say there's something like a ghost; something at the table, sitting next to my father, sitting on top of my father;

we're the stars, this summer, of the shore; we open up our throats to drink; we drink whatever is poured in our cups; we don't care if things get mixed; like brown drinks mixed with clear; like clear drinks mixed with wine; we don't care whose shirt we're wearing; whose car we're in; whose boat; we're the girls, this summer, everyone wants; and we dance up on the guys; we dance up on the chairs; we tie cherry stems into knots with our tongues; we open our mouths to show you the perfectly knotted stems;

the girl who drowned was a local girl; she was no one we knew well; we knew her tan lines when she wore a dress; we knew what they said about her; she was a knockout, they said; the guys all said; even my father said she was a knockout; but she wasn't that bright, my father said; so there was no one to blame, he said, for her drowning, but her;

but I often wonder about that night; I often think about that girl; I save the word *killers* under my tongue;

some nights, I lie back and close my eyes; I can feel their weight above me; I can feel, in the good way, like a girl; and then I can feel in the bad way; I send my brain to other thoughts, while my body lies there, pretending; I think about light and the speed of light; I think about black holes; and how there's no right side up or upside down in outer space; there's no sound on the moon;

near the end of the ride to the shore was the water; and from then on, it was only the water; my father was silent; my mother slept through it; but I was impressed, I now can admit; it was something to do with its size, or its depth; by depth I only mean physical; though one might make a case for another kind, a holy kind;

they're polished, these guys, so we followed them, like dogs, to the dock; now we dangle our legs off the edge; they throw their cigarettes into the water; they throw crushed cans, and I think some things; like how we're not the kind to throw shit in; but we're not the kind to say, Don't throw that shit; when the cans hit the water, the guys say, What; we say, What, and look to the other side; the other side is the poor side; it's a strip of dirty beach; it's weathered motels tilted into a road; it's beaten-up houses and couches on the lawns; it's the jetty the locals hang out on; we're not supposed to go to that side; but we're not sup-posed to do so many things; our demographic is confusing; all the expectations, all their opposites;

there are mountains on the moon tall as the ones on earth; but they're terrible, treeless; gray and dust; thinking of them, I can scare myself; I can see myself floating there;

at the ends of nights, we're under a tree or in a boat or in a bed and taken home; our makeup isn't what it was; our clothes are twisted; our shoes are somewhere; there are girls who walk us to find our shoes; these are younger girls who want to be us; they're our shadows and we hate them;

mornings, my father slams his fork to the table; he pounds the table so that everything shakes; he tries his best to stare me down; but I've perfected a better stare; I practice it, nights, on the younger girls; I can make my eyes go completely flat; it's terrifying how I look;

the guys have ways to make us give them what they want; they look directly at our mouths; they touch our hair and say it feels so soft; You smell like something I want to eat, they say; You smell like strawberries, they say; they ask us things to make us feel smart; they say, What would you do for a thousand dollars; they say, Would you steal a boat; they say, Would you kill someone; they say, Would you sleep with us; their mouths are at our ears; we're like a thousand dollars; we try not to laugh; they're becoming disappointing; at the boathouse, we wanted to be with these guys; now, with these guys, we want to be at the boathouse; this is a grass-is-greener situation; it has to do with perspective; like how the water from afar is one thing; the water up close is another; like how a body from afar is something; and a body from inside that body is something else;

the younger girls would sense the potential danger; they would run back to their houses before things got too wild; their parents would wake and make them tea; but my parents are sleeping their deep drugged sleep; my parents are sleeping each at his or her edge of the bed;

the younger girls still think about love as arrows through hearts; and please, girls; I know about love; I know what it is; just tiny motors whirring in one's saddest, darkest parts;

we often drink what's left in cans; we smoke what's left on the ground; we don't care if we look like trash; if our shirts come off; our shorts come off; when we dance like this, it means more than dancing; when we tie cherry stems into knots with our tongues; when we're found in a boat and crying and can't tell you why;

we say, We would sleep with you for a million dollars; But not for a thousand, we say; I realize how fucked up we sound; like what are we, total whores; then it's one thing to another fast; we only want the one thing; we only want some of that thing; we're willing to let them kiss us; we'll let them go up our shirts; but that's not good enough for them; because it hurts, they say, not to get off; it can go right to their brains, they say; it can fuck them up for good;

so they must have forgotten who we are; that we're the tops of our classes; that we know how the body works; and the moment they know this was all a waste; and the moment we know they know; they make a sound to represent agony; the sound reminds me of an animal from a show I saw as a child; they say, What the fuck is your problem; where do we start;

we know the universe is still expanding; we know we're shooting farther and farther out into what;

we know the sun will, at some point, collapse; that the earth will be burned to dust;

I tried, once, to explain these things in detail to my parents; my mother said, What's she talking about; my father: Hell if I know;

we stand to leave these guys on the dock; Just kill me, I say, as we walk; Just kill me, we say, and they're running to us; for a second, I think love; but now we're whipping through the air like trash; we're over their shoulders and spinning; they say they're going to throw us in; we're screaming, Put us down; I'm screaming, Fucking killers; and it's the world through speed, all split, all blurred; and it's all our fault for being such stars; for being such whores;

one night, we were on the dock, and there she was, holding a shoe in each hand; my father says she wasn't bright; and she wasn't, if you think of bright as top of your class; but if you think of bright, instead, as light; she was laughing out her words; something about some guys acting wild on the jetty; I could see her remember how wild they were; I could see her through the guys' eyes, my father's eyes; that night, I became her shadow, and she never even knew;

at the table, I stare my father down; I'm terrifying with my stare; it's like I'm stuck in some kind of trance; then everything is fractured; and it's a hundred forks; a hundred fathers; a hundred mothers saying, What's her problem; a hundred fathers saying, Go to hell;

we're spinning, and all I can think is water; I think of how cold it'll be; I think of how hard we'll hit; I think of how far it is to the bottom; and what I would miss above; not my mother and father's fucked-up shit; not the younger girls who wish so bad they were us; not these beautiful, agonized guys;

I would miss the feeling of everyone looking at us; of every-one laughing at us; the feeling, after, of sleeping it off;

I would miss the next-day feeling of starting again; of bare-foot, getting something to eat;

and don't think we're just teases; I also think about getting them off; I think about putting my hand on them; I think about putting my mouth on them; I think about lying under them; I don't even need to be good at it; I don't even need to look;

the ride back to the city will take me farther and farther from what I am; I'll lie across the back seat thinking, God;

were I in charge, the summer would go backward; we would start out split and end up not;

were I in charge, I would lie alone on the dock and feel the tiny motors whir while staring out at stars;

there's a moment, spinning, when spinning feels like being still; and I remember how I spun on the lawn, summers, when I was younger; I remember how hard the earth pulled me down; how when I finally stood, the grass stayed flat in the shape of me; and the grass would rise as I walked away; and I would grow too old for this game;

so do they throw us in; do we slowly sink; does light stop; does sound change; is it suddenly cold; do we feel the fish; the plants and trash; the sharp edge of a crushed can;

does the girl who drowned swim back to us; is she a knockout
still; do we love her still; do we love her enough to stay;

or do we push to the top; do we burst face first; are we a miracle;
or the opposite; predictable; do we lie under them on the dock;

because there's no sound on the moon, I often think about
screaming on the moon; I think about what it would be to
open my mouth and push out a scream I can feel but not hear;

because there's no right side up or upside down in outer space,
I often, when looking at the sky, feel I'm dangling above it;

what I mean is, girls, there is no love the way you think of love;

what I mean is, girls, I'm sorry;

in the show I saw when I was a child, an animal was running on dirt; I was supposed to be watching something else;
I wasn't supposed to be watching; I was supposed to be doing
my homework; there were things to learn; the beginnings and
ends of worlds to understand;

but someone had turned on this show; and I couldn't look
away; a guy's voice was saying things; his voice was getting
louder; there was a giant orange sun; a leafless tree; the animal running fast on the dirt; the animal running faster; this
animal on that animal;

Stars

; I'll say the setting is the boathouse; the setting is a washroom; the setting: night and summer; I'll say raining and
raining all week; I'll say the color of the walls; the color of my
hair; the color of her hair; our heights, our weights; say there's
no such thing as fiction; say there's only substitution; there's
only this standing in for that; and her standing in for another
her; and her for another and so on; say there's nothing to do at
night in rain; the guys get drunk and play billiards; the girls
get drunk and watch; some nights, we make up games; some
nights, the games are drinking; other nights, they're dares; on
this night, the game is piercing our ears through the hardest
part of the ear; it's the girl's idea to do this; she's done it before
to girls, she says, at her school; and it'll only hurt, she says, for
a flash; I have to wonder about the word *flash*; like is it a thing

now, *flash*; like are the girls at her school now using that word; the girls at my school are not; I say, Flash, and slow to make her feel dumb; so this is where everything starts; the setting: the edge of the tub; the setting: rain hitting the window; and sitting still so not to fall in; and a girl standing in for me; and a girl standing in for everything else; this girl who is now the girl in charge; this girl who won't be for long; she holds ice to my ear to numb it; she pinches to see if I can feel it; I tell her I can and what the fuck is she even doing, no warning; we can hear the guys in the billiards room; sometimes she plays the guys; sometimes she even beats them; she thinks it makes her look good; I think it makes her look like a guy; and the guys don't want us looking like them; they want us looking small and weak; to the guys, I like to seem small and weak; to the girls, I like to seem something else; to the girls, I like to seem terrifying; like a supernova; like the ends of their sad little worlds; but I close my eyes to be alone; I focus on the sound of the ice; it sounds like the dull crush of something coming through snow; winter is just a few months away; and the world of winter, of snow and school and long nights, is hard to think of in summer; I say, It sounds like snow, then wish I hadn't said it; it sounded sentimental; I can feel regret so immediately; every word we speak, these days, is such a risk; she says, Snow, and slow, and now I feel dumb; so I open my eyes and look at her face; one of her eyes is bigger than the other; I sense it'll get even bigger as she gets older; I'll hold this observation like a secret; I can make this observation work, in the future, in my favor; but for now, I close my eyes again; and she pinches my ear again; and before I can tell her I feel it still, she sticks the needle through my ear, straight through to the other side; the pain is like a light; I say, God; I want, now, to destroy her; I want to tell her what she is; so much lesser than me; so much dimmer; but I just sit here taking it; I've become so good at faking my way through every painful thing; I say, Your turn; but she's sliding down the wall now; she says, I'm too fucked up, and slides down to the floor; she says, Your ear; she says, You're absolutely gushing; her head droops to her shoulder; she has such a look on her face; and I think to get the guys right now; I could show them how sad she looks; but I'm not yet that kind of girl; I still feel things way too much; I mean I can feel the tiles against her back; I can feel the floor against her legs; I can feel the rain hit hard at the window; when I hear something coming through snow, I feel the cold of walking though snow; it doesn't matter what comes through it: a plow, a dog, a stranger coming up the walk; I can feel the entire world around me like a pulse; like a house I've never lived in; inside my ear is pounding; like hundreds of footsteps all at once; like the hallways at school, and school will soon start; and how terrible it always feels at first; how terrible, my uniform; terrible, my double life; to be one girl in the classroom; to be one girl in the washroom; to forget at times which one is which; there will come a night at the end of summer; the setting: the same; the conflict: the same; but this time, the girl will pull a nail from her pocket; this time, the game will be to drag the nail up each other's arms; I'll plan, again, that night, just to take it; and not to care about the pain; and not to care about the scar; to wear it inside my uniform that winter like a badge; to show it to the girls at school and say it was more than just a game; say it was more an initiation; more a secret club; that night, I won't even look at her face as she drags the nail up my arm; I'll look, instead, at the easy way my arm opens up toward her;

it'll feel cold then hot like any pain; it'll feel hot then hotter like any thrill; like any shame that replaces a thrill; then the thrill, again, of the shame; I'll say, Your turn, but she'll say, I'm bored; she'll say, I'm done, and look toward the door; so I'll never drag that nail up her arm; but I'll now know, watching the dark line spread on mine, that I have to overthrow her; I have to become the one in charge; I hope you can understand this; it's just a transfer of power; some law of physics; some conservation; there will come nights when I wish to have this power back; when I'm small and weak and some guy says, Your eyes; some guy says, Come on; then tells me where to put my hand; then tells me where to put my mouth; then tells me what will happen if I don't; but not what will happen if I do; no warning of that feeling of dirt; no warning that feeling of buried alive; and the girl in the classroom is totally dead; that girl pushing up her sleeve like a pro; the scar on her arm she'll never be able fully to hide; and, Did it hurt, the girls will say; Of course it fucking hurt, I'll say; And what did you do, the girls will say; What do you think I did, I'll say; but you know I won't go after her with the nail; I'll never be that kind of girl; so I'll only grab her hair and pull and hard; it'll be like pulling a string on a talking doll; like pulling a tail on a dog; her head will jerk in a blur before me; she'll make a sound I'll be surprised by; I won't have expected a sound at all; but I'll terrify her for a second; I'll look like something she hasn't, before this, seen; and I'll see her see it, what I am; a fucking force; a massive star; and she'll always be a minor star; a proto-star; so everything, then, will start to shift; so everything will, eventually, be mine; let's call this *climactic moment*; let's call this big, my God; but first, you have to be nothing; first, you have to sit on the edge of that tub; first, you have to feel the needle pushing slowly through; and the small explosions in your ear; and the gushing down your neck you think won't stop; first, you have to consider the weakness of calling for help; I know if I call, the guys will rush in to save me; because they love me at my weakest; so I open my mouth to scream; but then she's laughing, sitting on the washroom floor; her teeth are fucking perfect; her eyes are absolutely charming; I want to tell her I love her eyes; I want to sit closer to her; I want to rest my head on hers; I want to let her pull my self into her self; because this isn't the night to overthrow her; this isn't the night to be in charge; because on this night, I'm still pretending; I'm still insisting what lies beneath every wrecked human body is good;

Liars

Our father says not to say *gone to shit*.

When people ask, and they will, our father says, you should not say *gone to shit*.

But the guys were staring down into the water. The girls were holding each other's arms. They were screaming into each other's hair the way those girls all would.

It was total shit, my brother says.

Our father says, What did I say.

We're in our father's study. Our father's study is a replica of our father's other study. But this one, because it's at the shore, has seascapes on the walls. It has old maps on the walls. Our father's other study, because it's in the city, has pictures on the walls of the city.

Our father and my brother are sitting in leather chairs.

They're the same kind of chair as the chairs in our father's other study. They're each on one side of the desk. I'm sitting on the floor.

Our father says, Were you drunk.

Were you high, our father says.

Our father is being a certain way we've never liked. There's nothing to do when he's being like this. So my brother just sits there, arms folded across his front.

Our father says not to say he was high.

Not even a little, our father says.

My brother looks at me like our father is such a dumbass. He looks at me like what does it mean to be a little high. There's no such thing as a little high. You're either high, or you're not high.

Our father says, People are going to ask.

They'll ask, he says, what you were doing.

They'll ask, he says, what you were on.

So he says to say it was just a party.

Just a party, he says, with friends.

But my brother says, We wouldn't call it a party.

No one would call it that, he says.

You don't know what you're saying, he says.

My brother is right that we wouldn't use the word *party*. A party is a different thing, a structured thing. This we would just call *hanging out*. This we would just call *partying*.

So I say to our father, The word you want is *partying*.

Our father looks at me for the first time today. He looks at me like where did you even come from.

Still looking at me, he says to my brother not to use the word *partying*.

Partying, says our father, implies something other than a party.

Partying, he says, is not the same thing as a party.

People, our father says, have already begun to talk.

And these people, our father says and shakes his head like you better watch it.

This is one of our father's tricks for wearing people down. We've fallen for this trick before. And people at the boathouse, too, have fallen. And people at his business, too. They call him boss, and they call us mister and miss.

One day, our father's business will be my brother's. So for now, my brother, our father says, needs to straighten up. He needs to get his act together, our father says. He needs to learn to fake it, he says, the way the people here all do.

But my brother says there's nothing to fake. He wasn't even there when it happened, he says. He was pissing in the trees, he says. And when he got back to the dock, everything, he says, had gone to fucking shit.

Our father is staring my brother down.

He says, Why didn't you piss in the water.

Guys always piss in the water, he says.

And people are going to ask, he says, why you had to piss on a tree.

He looks at me like what the hell is wrong with your brother. I look at him like how the hell do I know.

My brother says, I didn't have to piss on a tree.

He says, I just didn't want to piss right there.

Not in front of the girls, he says.

Excuse me, he says, for not taking out my fucking dick in front of the girls.

I realize my brother is being serious. That nothing could be more serious than this. I mean we're talking about a girl who drowned. But we're talking without any feeling. So I'm not yet feeling is what I'm saying. And I'm immature I'm also saying. So I'm too immature not to laugh at the word *dick*. I can't not laugh at *fucking dick*.

Our father looks at me again.

He says to my brother, Why is she here.

He says to my brother, Tell her to get the hell out.

This is another one of our father's tricks. He's trying to get my brother to take his side in a war against me. My brother has fallen for this one before. So many times they've laughed in my face. They've made me feel like the lowest thing.

But today, our father's trick won't work. My brother's head is somewhere else. He's turned to face the window. And it's here he'll face from this point on.

Last night, my brother didn't come home. None of us even noticed. We just went to bed, woke in the morning, sat at the table.

Then my brother walked in looking like he'd been dug up from the dirt.

Our father said, Well, look who's here.

My brother said nothing, went to his room.

Our father went back to eating.

But you could tell there was something up. You could tell by the speed at which my brother was moving. The quiet way he closed his door.

Tonight, I'll find out how my brother, after, wandered around all night. I'll find this out from one of my brother's friends. He'll say my brother sat in people's boats. He sat in trees in people's yards. They found him at the market, late, lying in the empty lot.

I'll ask if he was sleeping, but who cares if he was, my brother's friend will say.

Now my brother is looking at something past the window. Like something he wants to move toward. Like he'll step right through to some other world. And I've dreamed this too. Some holy world, and I've wanted it bad.

Now I'm worried that my brother is done. That our father is too. That we'll leave the room and never get back to this night.

But my brother says, I can prove I wasn't on the dock.

He says, I remember the tree I pissed on.

It had a giant knot, this tree, he says.

And I pissed, he says, on that giant knot.

At first, I imagine the tree. The knot in the tree like some kind of face.

Then, I imagine the girl who drowned. She's the only local girl there. The local girls hang out on the jetty. They don't hang out on the dock. The other girls want her to leave. But she's too fucked up. So she's doubled over laughing. No, she's doubled over crying. Now she's falling down, now falling in. And I should be feeling something.

But it's like watching a movie of a girl who drowned. A movie of guys talking about a girl.

You know what you sound like, our father says.

You sound like a liar, he says.

He says, This is what liars sound like.

This is another trick we know. My brother should just ignore it.

But he says, Fuck you.

I'm not lying, he says.

And our father says, I'm not saying you're lying.

I'm saying, our father says, that you sound like a fucking liar.

Our father and I were at the table when the cop knocked at the door. Our father told me to go somewhere else. But I stayed right where I was.

So the cop and our father walked outside. I could still hear some of what they said. The cop said it was late. The kids were on the dock. The girl was in her underwear.

Our father said, Her underwear.

Then they walked away, farther across the lawn.

The thing is, we often swim in our underwear. We also swim in nothing. It depends on who's on the dock. And what our bodies look like. And what our underwear looks like.

So I imagine how this girl would have swum. I mean was she stripping down to nothing. Or had she stripped down as far as she meant to strip down.

I mean did she go into the water before she meant to go in.

Like was she pushed is what I mean.

Tonight, I'll ask my brother's friend what really happened.

He'll laugh and mess up my hair.

Just tell me, I'll say.

Just tell me, he'll say, in a voice that's supposed to sound like mine.

Then he'll wrestle me to the grass.

I've seen our father wear my brother down for less than this. The smallest scratch on the car. Not walking the dog. I've seen him nearly bring my brother to tears for so much less.

But my brother is back in that other world. And now I'm

part there too. And I could stay there too. I could stay there forever, pretending.

In the future, I'll feel it all. It'll start on a night this summer. I'll be walking past the dock with some kids, and I swear I'll see her ghost.

So I'll scream, and the kids will say, What the fuck, and I'll point and say, It's her.

And they'll throw me into the water for being fucked up.

Now our father is looking at me.

Now he winks at me, and this means something.

It means my role has changed.

He says, What the hell is wrong with your brother.

What guy, he says, would leave the girls to piss on a tree.

What guy, he says, and I don't yet realize what he's asking me to do.

I mean I realize he wants me to take his side in a war against my brother.

But I don't yet realize, he wants me to objectify these girls.

To imagine these girls as solely bodies.

And to imagine these girls as solely bodies, I must imagine my own body as something else.

Like a field covered in snow. Like a spread of clouds. A pile of dirt.

So forgive me for where I go with this. Forgive me for the crazy shit now going through my head.

For thinking I'm now our father's son. That the business, one day, will be mine. That people will call me boss. That I'll never again be miss.

Forgive me for forgetting we're talking about an actual girl who drowned.

In her underwear, I say and laugh.

What kind of guy, I say.

Tonight, I'll get too fucked up.

My brother's friend will tell me things.

Like that everyone was on the dock.

Like that my brother was on the dock.

And the girl had gotten way too wild.

So what happened, I'll say.

She fell, he'll say.

That's it, he'll say.

And she drowned.

I have a chance now to be useful. To pull the truth out of my brother. And if the truth is my brother was there on the dock, if the truth is my brother was high, if the truth is my brother just lost his shit, that he pushed her in, that he held her under, or knows who did, then our father will twist that truth into a lie that will save my brother's ass.

I say to my brother, What kind of guy, but my brother is covering his ears with his hands.

I've only seen him do this once before. This isn't what I want to remember right now. Lunch in a restaurant with our father. A fancy room, and we're way too small for this place.

There are white cloths and white plates and vines growing on the walls.

And because I'm young and because I already hate so much, I dare my brother to pour a glass of water over his head.

Our father says to me, Don't start.

He says to my brother, Don't.

But my brother pours the water. It all happens so fast. I'm amazed by how wet his face is. How wet and flat his hair is. These ladies near us are laughing. And at first, we're laughing too. But then my brother covers his ears. Because he has to shut them out, these ugly old ladies laughing at him.

Well, all of this is irrelevant. Our father dragging my brother outside. Then me just sitting alone at that table. Me sitting there like a grown-up. Staring these ugly old bitches down.

The night I see the girl's ghost, it won't be that. It'll just be me too fucked up. And a shadow, a light. Some peripheral thing moving about.

But I'll feel the loss you feel when waking from a dream that's better than your life.

So I'll scream. I mean I'll scream like crazy.

So the kids will throw me in.

But I won't drown that night. I'll rise to the top the way a body can.

Now I say to my brother, What happened last night.

Just tell us what happened, I say.

This isn't one of our father's tricks.

He has better tricks than being direct.

I can feel our father's disappointment.

I've totally fucked this up.

Our father's face, you don't want to see it.

And my brother's face you don't want to see.

Our father says, You're done.

He points to the door, says, Go.

It's easy to imagine the guys staring into the water. To imagine the girls losing their shit. The summer cops not knowing where to start. Then the real cops come and tell everyone go the fuck home.

But it's harder to imagine my brother. To imagine where he's standing.

Or how he's standing. Or what he's wearing.

Or if he jumped in. If he pulled her out.

If he pushed the wet hair from her face.

If he pressed his mouth to her mouth.

If he breathed as hard as he could.

If she jumped back to life for a second.

Our father says, I'm counting to three.

But forget about that dumbass.

I'm walking out of his study.

I'll go the boathouse and find my brother's friend.

He'll be smoking with some guys.

He'll mess up my hair like I'm a child.

He'll pin me to the grass.

I often imagine a life just wandering around. I imagine living in boats or in trees or riding trains across the world.

And how hard I've tried, since, to have this life. How many times I've walked a street unknown and wanting to stay unknown.

But how hard it is to fully shed the fucked-up thing you've always been.

To know you'll always be this fucked-up thing, no matter what.

Dumb and drunk on the grass.

Tracing shadows on his face.

You whisper, Tell me, into his ear.

He whispers into your mouth.

Machines

if I never learned the earth was spinning;
that there was no bottom and there was no top;
that light from stars I could see left years before I could see
the light;
that so many stars could now be gone;
that the sun, one day, as well, would be;
that this wasn't the kind of thing to overthink;
and if I never learned to overthink;
if I could switch thoughts off before they started to spin;
take that first celebrity suicide;
I mean the first one in our lives;
he wrote a note then shot himself;
we weren't supposed to hear this;

they were whispering so we wouldn't;

it was our mother and a neighbor from down the street;

we called her aunt, but she wasn't our aunt;

she was these kids' mother, and we hated her kids;

we hated her more;

she made our mother act so dumb;

she made her drink too much;

they were drinking, this day, a bottle of orange liqueur;

the bottom of the bottle was shaped like an orange;

it was our fake aunt's bottle she brought over;

it was too early to be drinking liqueur;

our fake aunt was often drunk in the day;

she was divorced, and divorce, back then, meant something;

it meant fucked-up kids and it meant your reputation;

it meant our fake aunt fell down, drunk, on her way home from our house;

but that was a different day;

that day, she fell over the hose the help had left in a bunch on the lawn;

we heard her scream, and it could have been from anything, a scream like that;

my brother and I ran outside to see;

our fake aunt was facedown in the grass;

we didn't want to touch her, so we waited for her to get to her knees, figure it out;

our mother didn't drink in the day unless our fake aunt was at our house;

our mother was weak around other women, and we'd always known she was weak;

now here she was, pretending not to be drunk, pretending an interest in us we knew was just pretend;

then, Pow, our fake aunt said and stood and shaped her
hand like a gun at her head;
What, we said;
our mother said, Nothing;
to our fake aunt, she said, The kids;
our mother never once thought before she spoke;
she always ruined it all;
my brother said, Why the gun;
Tell me, he said;
I said, Tell me;
there was no reason to keep a secret from us;
we knew too much already;
there were bigger things than the things they kept a secret;
like all of space, for instance;
like all I knew about space;
like how spaceships floated in a free fall;
how astronauts floated within them;
how weightlessness wasn't like floating in water;
it wasn't a calming thing;
how a single force could push you out of orbit;
it could send you to the darkest place;
because you've never had control;
you've always had to pretend it;
now here we all were, in a kitchen, pretending;
here we all were, as if nothing;
we were about to leave for a party;
it was a bowling party for some kid we didn't like;
the bowling alley was on the other side;
our father drove us and told us, Be good;
I wasn't sure if he meant be good at bowling;
or if he meant be good in some other way;

there were holy ways we were never taught, but heard about;

certain kids who knew this stuff, kids we would never be;

they were kids our mother always called good;

but we preferred the asshole kids we hated;

this party was full of assholes;

my brother bowled, but I sat at the counter;

I liked the pizza the bowling alley had;

I liked the local guys who served the pizza, because they also served me beer;

this was because of how I looked;

I didn't care what the reason was;

I was learning to work with what I had;

so I sat there, feeling old;

I drank beer from a cup meant for soda;

there was music I liked coming from the walls;

and the sounds of all those crashing pins;

like the sound of gravity, I thought, then thought it seemed insane;

like how a crush makes you think, or just drinking does;

but I didn't care then there were things in space that couldn't move out of our way;

I didn't care then what asteroid struck us, what black hole sucked us closer to its edge;

pretty soon, the other kids were at the counter;

they were talking the shit kids always talked;

all of them going on and on;

that first celebrity suicide;

they said he'd shot himself in the head;

they said it happened in a kitchen;

so then I was seeing our kitchen table;

then I was seeing our mother and the bottle shaped like an orange;

then I was seeing our dumb fake aunt, her hand like a gun at her head;

like she was better than him, which she was not;

like she was better than anyone, but she was the absolute worst;

there was a night she came by our house with a dog;

we were eating dinner, and she walked in like she lived there;

she held up the dog with one hand and said, Does anyone want a dog;

my brother and I said, We do;

we said, We want that dog;

but our mother said no to getting the dog;

she said no way were we getting a dog when we couldn't even help around the house;

we looked at each other like what did that even mean;

none of us ever helped around the house;

we had help to help around the house;

our mother was just pretending again;

but our fake aunt was better at this;

this dog was the runt of its litter, she said, and it was the only one that wasn't brown;

this dog was gray, she said, and it was the only one with longer hair;

her kid, she whispered behind her hand, had kicked it across a room;

because his parents were divorced is what we thought, and now he was all fucked up;

divorce meant that, and it meant our fake aunt was all
dressed up for going out;
    there was a way one dressed for going out;
    there was a way one smelled, so obvious, so desperate;
    our mother said, I said no;
    but our father was petting the dog now;
    he had one arm around our fake aunt's waist;
    he made sounds into the dog's fur;
    don't turn this into a thing;
    our fake aunt wasn't the one;
    we hated her, but she wasn't the one we hated the absolute
most;
    and whether or not we got to keep the dog;
    it doesn't matter the outcome of that day;
    that scene in our kitchen doesn't matter;
    or any scene in our kitchen;
    or in any kitchen, or in any room;
    as if rooms could even protect us;
    as if the sun would never collapse;
    and we would just go on forever;
    obeying some law of inertia;
    a ball rolling straight down the lane;
    no force coming in to stop it;
    there was such dumb hope in those laws;
    such bullshit in those laws;
    because the ball would eventually hit the pins;
    it would send them wild across the floor;
    the pins would eventually hit the walls;
    a kid would press a small white button;
    a machine would sweep the pins away;
    a machine would reset the pins;

and the whole fucking thing would start over;
that celebrity we loved because he was hot;
and by hot I mean more than looks;
the kids were acting like no big deal;
but I felt I was being emptied;
then I felt a shadow moving in;
like the shadow of something you can't even see;
or something you're not supposed to;
my brother kept asking questions;
he wanted details no one else did;
I could see the chewed-up pizza on his tongue;
I said, Close your mouth;
he said, What's your problem;
I said, Close your fucking mouth;
what was I even thinking then;
it's hard to explain, I guess;
astronauts again, I guess;
forced travel through unfamiliar space;
nearly everything in it unreachable;
everything in it no better than anything else;
just hydrogen to helium;
just helium to something else;
and something else to something else;
so what good, I learned that day, was hot;
what good, I learned, was celebrity;
I'd always wanted to have it;
I often imagined, late at night, my entourage, my limousine,
my attitude;
I often tried to will this future for myself;
though could I even believe in this future;
or could I only believe in the grander one, the destined one;

the temporary free fall;

the on and on, then off;

no wonder the kids shot at their heads, stuck out their
tongues, fell to the ground, laughing;

we were all just so confused;

there were times I wanted nothing more than to break free
from our orbit;

I wanted a force to come in, already, and upset it;

I'd been secretly holding on, I admit, to the hope of this
force coming in;

not an asteroid force or a black hole force;

but the slightest shred of holy;

some shred of belief that everything would be revealed;

that the world was something conceivable;

a linear path directed toward some good;

but there would be more celebrity suicides;

and noncelebrity suicides;

and more explosion and more expansion;

how could you not overthink it;

but the kids got back to bowling;

the guy at the counter poured me another beer;

I wasn't going to drink this one;

I'd already outgrown this moment;

I called our mother, said, Come get us;

but our father came instead;

my brother put up a fight out front;

he wanted to keep bowling, he said;

he was beating the other kids, he said;

he was now, my brother, officially, the enemy;

we were staring each other down across an invisible line;

in the car, our father didn't talk;

my brother sighed again and again and again;
some old song played on the radio;
what was out the car window passed too fast;
I couldn't focus on any of it;
all those houses whooshing by;
and all that grass;
and all those trees;
all those birds;
all those stars;

Saviors

she always rides fast when the boardwalk is empty; but it's not empty, really; it's just not what it is at night; it's just not what it is with crowds and lights and the smells of grease and sweat and smoke; and the screaming from the rides; the screaming from the games; the step-right-up; the rifle shots; the balloons on the tops of plastic clown heads filling with water so some dumb fuck can win a stuffed toy that isn't even worth the price of the ticket you need to play the game;

she always rides fast, her hair flying back so it tangles in a way we call beachy; it's a way we call just-fucked; it's a way we all want our hair to look and can't always get it just right; we use soap on it; we use salt in it; we use cooking oil and suntan oil;

and at the place where my brother's friend goes to eat, he always pulls at her tangled hair; he says things like, Rough night; like, Did you get some; he punches his fist into his palm; and she always laughs when he's being like this; when he's being a dick;

my brother's friend once won a tiny stuffed dog for knocking over a pyramid of cans; and even though it was ragged, dirty, missing an ear, and my brother's friend pretended to fuck it, she wanted to keep it and tied it by its legs to the back of her bike where it flaps up and up, faster as she goes faster;

we're also into my brother's friend; but we're into him only sometimes; we've both hooked up with him on the dock; and in a sitting room in the boathouse; and in a guest room in the boathouse; and once, just for one of us, on a boat;

but today isn't about my brother's friend; because last night wasn't about him; it was only about us getting fucked up; and we're still fucked up; so we're walking the boardwalk in search of food; and the sun is too bright; and the smells and the sounds; this isn't our greatest day;

now imagine two kids on opposite sides of the boardwalk; the kids are locals, you can tell; it's the way they style their hair; it's the way they dress and the way they stand; it's a small kid and a big kid; the big kid has a bruise on his face; the small kid looks like he never eats; he's all ribs jutting out and hip bones; he's a face like the skull of a bird;

now imagine the kids stretching a wire, high, across the boardwalk; imagine how someone walking along would walk into the wire and stop; can you see how funny that would be if you were the one who thought up this trick, if you were the one tightly holding the wire as someone walked in; and can you see how funny it would be if you were the one to walk into the wire; well, we do walk into that wire; we stumble right in like fucking drunks; it's funny to the local kids; it's funny, at first, to us; but it stops being funny at a certain point; our hangovers are too distracting; we're unable to have real fun;

but we can force ourselves to pull it together; we duck under the wire and say to the kids fuck off; we say we're done with this game, and fuck them for wasting our time; but the kids aren't looking in our direction; they're back in their places, the wire stretched tight;

this part is harder to describe; how it happens fast, but also in slow motion; how we see her in the distance; we see her riding down the boardwalk; and it's her hair all wild, her face like that; and we mean to run out, to tell her to stop; but our reflexes are super slow; it's like our reflexes are broken; like our reflexes have never worked; and she's unstoppable, besides; she's racing to see my brother's friend; she's determined to get there first; because if she's first, he can't call her a spy; he can't call her a stalker; and she'll sit at the counter; she'll order a soda; she'll wait, alone, until he walks in; and then what; no one knows what; there's just a way that love can fuck with you that hard; there's a way the things your body does are no longer up to you;

so imagine her riding right into the wire; imagine the kids losing their grip on the wire she's going so fast; imagine her flying, her bike crashing, the wire like a scarf flowing behind her; can you see her bike spinning away, the wheels on the bike still spinning; can you see how now we're paralyzed; how we're absolutely stuck in place; it's like we know we have to call for help; and we're saying we have to call; but no one is calling; we're just walking to her, slow as we can;

we're told in our schools to devise a master plan; by master, they mean pretend you're guys; by plan, they mean forever; our master plan, we decide, is science; we're atypical in this way; we're atypical for science kids; we're hotter than those kids; but like those kids, we need to know the reasons why; we need to know the numbers of; the fourteen billion years; the one hundred billion stars; the five-point-eight trillion miles;

last night, three planets in the sky, we looked from the boathouse lawn; we pretended we were just lying there; and had the guys walked over, we would have closed our eyes; but she was the one who walked over; she was the one now lying on the lawn, looking up; so we pointed to show her, perhaps to impress her; and she said, God; and we said, No; because she meant God, and we meant something else;

so we went inside the boathouse, and she stayed where she was; not because of the planets; not even because of God; it was just because of my brother's friend; and how sad how she was waiting; sad how she wasn't allowed in the boathouse; and was she even allowed on the lawn;

the kids with the wire are standing with us; there's something fucked up with the small kid; he says to the big kid, Is she dead;

on another day, this would make us laugh; on any other day, we would laugh our fucking heads off; the big kid says, Shut your mouth, and punches the small kid in the arm; but you can tell the big kid is scared; he didn't want to hurt this girl; meaning he didn't want to hurt a local girl; and the big kid is trying to figure out—you can tell by the way his eyes move—we've seen these eyes on guys before—whether to stay there or to run;

at times you want to ask for forgiveness; but you don't know forgiveness from what; and you don't know who you're asking it from; but at times you feel you've done something wrong; you feel the need to be absolved;

at times you want to press pause on this world, watch everything freeze, then wander around, punching the things you want to punch, and touching some other things;

her hair is spread around her face; she's looking up at our eyes; she says, I want my cigarettes; she says, I want my purse; but did she even have her purse with her; she says, I want my doll; we're like what the fuck doll does she mean; at first, we think she means the stuffed dog she's tied to the back of her bike; we untie it and hold it in front of her face; but the dog isn't what she wants; and time is moving weirdly again; and she's looking too much at our eyes; and she still looks hot, even lying there; and it's so fucked up to think this now; so it's time to acknowledge the cut; how much it's been gushing; how hard it is not to look;

last night, we said it wasn't God; we said no one was in control; we said things didn't happen for a reason; we said things happened because of mass and time and suns exploding; and a tilted planet, a spinning planet, a planet flying out and out;

like how this happened today because this girl was moving at a certain speed from a certain height at a certain time, and there was, as there always will be, a certain force;

like how eventually she'll have to rise; and eventually this day will end; and eventually, on another day, she'll drown;

the big kid tells the small kid to get help; he's taking off his shirt; he's handing the shirt to us; he says to hold the shirt to the cut; he's acting like he's in charge; like he's some kind of savior or something; but we're not falling for this gesture; we're just staring at his shirt; he says to take it and please; we're expected by him to do what he says; he's a guy, after all, local or not, and we're expected to listen to guys; but which one of us can touch that dirty shirt; and which one of us can touch the shirt to her; we're finding other things to do with our hands; we put them into pockets; we scratch at bites on our legs; we comb the knots out of our hair; so the big kid holds his shirt to her; so she holds his wrist;

last night, she just pointed to the sky and laughed—and not at us—she would never have laughed at us—but at something we'll never know;

we're not in love with my brother's friend; we just love when he lifts us and spins until we're laughing so hard we could die; we just want to be with him again with him looking at us the way he does; we want to feel that significant weight, his crushing fucked-up weight against our ribs;

this is a story about desperation; you could also say acceleration; but in this story, they're the same;

the doll she wants is a doll, she says, from when she was a kid; she'd left the doll in her yard, she says, and we say, There is no doll; but she's only talking to the big kid; she's holding his wrist and looking at him like do this for me; like you have to do this one thing; he's looking at us like what should I do; we're looking at him like this is all yours; like this is your thing you started; we say again, There is no doll; but she's only talking to the kid; the doll's limbs were chewed right off, she says; they were chewed ragged by a stray, she says; and she found it like that in the yard, she says; and her mother, she says, stitched it up;

it's hard not to be struck by her words; struck by her choices in this moment; because she's the one chewed ragged; she's the one who needs to be stitched; the doll is her, and how does she not see this;

so perhaps we're confusing terror with humor; and perhaps this says something bad about us; but we're so hungover we can't even think; so we're laughing now; and she says to stop laughing; and this makes us laugh even harder; so she says to the kid, This isn't funny; she says to the kid, This is real; This could have been them, she says to the kid; and she's right that this isn't funny; and she's right that this is real; but she's wrong that this could have been us;

it couldn't have been us because: one, we don't ride bikes; two, if we did ride bikes, we wouldn't ride that fast; three, we wouldn't be going to find my brother's friend in the day; four, we would never make our feelings known; five, we're not that desperate; six, we're not that dumb; and on and on and on;

our master plan is science; and by master we mean control the world; and by plan we mean control the world; and by science we mean fuck you;

we say, Get up; but she won't get up; she's mad at us, she says; we laughed at her, she says; and she wants her doll, she says; she says she'll stay there, and she'll die there, unless she gets her doll; she says to the kid God is punishing her; we roll our eyes so hard; she's done some things, she says to the kid; the kid says, What kind of things; but we don't give a shit what kind of things; she looks like she's about to cry; she says to the kid she just needs help; no shit she needs help; We're waiting for help, the kid says;

this is a story about salvation; but that doesn't mean this girl was saved; and it doesn't mean that we were saved; or that anyone was, or ever would be; it only means that something, in this moment, needed saving;

at times you just want to keep pause pressed; you want the planet's spinning to stop; you want to stop rushing into space; you want a second to think about things; or not to think about things; just a second to pull it together; to understand your sad desire; this sad force;

at times you just want to surrender to holy, to fall to your knees—we've seen this surrender in this girl before—in front of it all;

my brother's friend is walking toward us; there are girls in bikinis walking behind him; the younger girls who want to be us; typical girls like we once were; my brother's friend doesn't see her yet; he sees us, though, so we pretend we don't see him; we're trying to look better than we feel; we're trying for something like casual, something like beautiful; he points his fingers at us like a gun; his shoulders look so wide;

he came to the boathouse late last night; by then, we were just a drunken mess; we said, Where have you been; he said, What do you care; we said, Don't you love us; he said, What; then that look in his eyes we know too well; then he walked outside, and we watched from the window; we watched him find her on the lawn; we weren't spying on them; don't think we were; we just watched him lie down next to her; and were they holding hands; and was that God punishing us;

when you're with him, nights, it's first like flying; it's then like crashing again and again;

then, after, you're back in your normal orbit; you can feel an entire revolution;

then, after, alone on your back, looking up at some star, some ceiling, some flash of thought, it's like being punched in the gut and punched in the gut and punched in the gut;

so you're driven right up to the line of violence; you can feel your fingernails cutting into your palms;

so you drink what's left; so you find your friends; how it always goes; the guys being guys; the girls being girls; the girls being guys;

the night on the boat was different though; it was different because of the boat; it was tied to the dock; but it felt like we were floating farther out there, somewhere;

no, the night was different because he stuck around; so I stuck around until it was light; and then everything was the same;

this is a story about forgiveness; because I've done some things; and what kind of things; does it even matter what kind;

at times I want to fall to my knees; I want to stay on my knees;

and at other times I want billions of years and trillions of miles of something real;

now everything is going too fast; a summer cop running toward us; my brother's friend running toward us; and his face has changed to serious; so this is serious now; so he pushes us out of the way like we're guys;

now everything is so sad; the big kid looking smaller now; the small kid holding the stuffed dog now; he's petting it now, and I'm scared for these kids; so I say to these piece of shit local kids, Run; I say, Now;

so it's the big kid outrunning the small kid; the small kid running like a girl;

it's the cop bent over her body; my brother's friend bent over her body;

it's the girls in bikinis whispering; these girls now looking at us and please; you do not want to look at us today; you do not want to be like us today; because we're not the saviors in this story; we would have let her die there;

Animals

were it not just things standing in for other things;

were it not just me cast in the role of idealized me;

were, growing up, our father's portrait not above the piano no one played but him;

were it a grand piano so the portrait made more sense, but we weren't that kind of rich;

we were another kind of rich, which is to say new money, meaning barely money compared to old;

but were we not performing old money in a brand-new-money house;

were there not portraits of other members of our family on other walls, though not portraits of us all;

when you cut your hair, he said to my brother, we'll get your portrait done;

when you gain some weight, he said to me;

the portraits were in our house in the city, not in our house at the shore;

our house at the shore was a lesser version of our house in the city, a number of rooms, a piano, as well;

our house at the shore had no portrait above the piano, but a painted seascape that looked nothing like the sea;

our father called the seascape redundant;

he called it an obligation;

perhaps it was above the piano at our house at the shore where our portraits, mine and my brother's, would have gone, had they ever been made;

it wasn't a big deal to me that they weren't;

it wasn't until several years later that I even remembered there was talk of these portraits that never got made;

because several years later, when I was in college, I was with a guy whose portrait hung above his bed;

he said a well-known painter had painted it;

he said this well-known painter had said to him, I would love to paint your portrait;

I cared less about who painted the portrait, and more about where it hung;

because I wasn't sure, at first, if I could be with a guy whose portrait hung above his bed;

but the guy was old money, and the rules were different;

and we got drunker, and he got his way;

this isn't a story, besides, about my thing with this guy, which was short-lived and is, now, nearly forgotten;

this is a personal history of not knowing where to look;

the choices, my God, we have to make;

take this scene in our house at the shore, for instance;

take my parents in this scene in our house at the shore;

it was breakfast, and our father, when he was around, would molest our mother, when she was around, at the stove in the kitchen every morning;

it wasn't every morning;

and is *molest* too strong a word for what he did;

is it too hard a thing to prove;

when one is so much bigger and so much smarter at seeming together;

when one is a tyrant, and the other is not;

and the other has been known to get carried away;

she has been known to carry on;

so it was our father's hands all over our mother, early mornings, at the stove, and I was trying to eat my eggs;

it was my brother moving food around and around on his plate;

it was the clicks of his fork, the scrapes of his fork, the sound of chewing I couldn't stand;

he never looked directly at the scene going on at the stove;

I couldn't help but look, though I knew it wasn't right;

and it wasn't right to think about it later, yet I did;

it wasn't right to play it back, our father's hands pushing our mother at the stove, our mother saying, Stop it, saying, I'll burn your eggs, our mother pushing our father away, pushing with her hands, her hips, our father holding tight and laughing in that way he often laughed;

like a guy getting his way again;

like the guy I wanted to be;

that dick I always wanted to be;

after he left, our father said to me and my brother, Your mother is ice;

he said, A block of ice, and positioned his hands as if holding a block of ice;

and what did we do;

we sat there I guess and laughed I guess;

but I had these dreams, I now can say, of fighting our father
until there was nothing left to fight;

they weren't sleep-dreams, really, but daydreams, and in
them I could really fuck him up;

this isn't to say I was violent;

I mean I wasn't inherently violent beyond a baseline kind
of violent;

I'd gotten up in faces before, but not with a fist up to the
face;

like all those times some girl fucked the guy I liked;

and all those guys I didn't like who checked me out;

all the locals who said such shit when I walked past;

and I was like what the fuck are you looking at;

I was like don't you fucking look at me;

the portrait of our father above the piano was him in a col-
lared shirt I'd never seen him wear, and the portrait of our
mother was her in a flowered dress I'd never seen her wear,
and the portrait of our dog, who we only owned for a short
time because he'd turned, in the words of our father, *wild*,
was him sitting up in a low-lit room I'd never seen;

the portrait of the guy I was with was him in a three-piece
suit, standing against a dark wall;

when I was in his bed, it was sometimes the portrait I
looked at;

this had to do with position;

I realize when I say position there are other ways to read it;

like one's position in life and all of that;

but I just mean he wanted me positioned in a certain way,
so he could watch me from below;

though this wasn't just about watching me, I later learned,
but watching his effect on me;

he would say things like, Do you like it like this, Do you
like it like this, Do you like it like this;

he would say things like, Look at me baby, I said look at
me baby, I said look at me;

my choices were look down at his face or look up at the
portrait;

and there was something about his strained face, his red
face, his working too hard to make me work hard too;

and there was something about the portrait;

so I often closed my eyes and put my mind somewhere else;

it was often somewhere in outer space;

it was orbiting the planets;

it was making shapes from stars;

it was a secret I had, my mind going out to some too cold
place, some too hot place;

I admit I got off on the secret;

it wasn't unusual, getting off on a secret;

it was the thing, I would guess, most gotten off on;

still, I made the clichéd sounds one makes;

as the headboard made its clichéd sounds;

and the bedsprings made their clichéd sounds;

as stars exploded in my mind into stars exploding into stars;

I sometimes thought of one of the locals from the shore;

he worked at the rides in the months that there were rides;

he looked like a star we liked;

like the poorest version of that star;

the girl and I would stand there staring at him;

she wanted him first, but I wanted him more;
with some guys it didn't matter;
like my brother's friends;
or guys who came in for a week;
with this guy, though, it was different;
our father said not to talk to the locals;
my brother was told not to let me;
Keep an eye on her, our father would say;
as if my brother's eye on me;
as if any guy's eye on me;
I mostly knew not to fight our father;
I mostly knew not to fight him, because our father would
have fought me back;
and I knew I would have lost that fight;
this wasn't molestation, a father fighting a daughter;
it was just a father fighting a daughter, that was all;
but our father pushing into our mother at the stove was
something else;
as was our mother pushing our father away and pushing
him away and pushing him away, as I would have, then, done,
to any guy who came at me like that, his hands too big like
that;
there was a time the eggs did burn;
another time, a skillet hit the kitchen floor;
it was just a regular pan for frying;
there's no reason to use the word *skillet*, which suggests a
domesticity that wasn't our kind;
it suggests a quaintness that wasn't our thing;
that pan hit the kitchen floor so hard;
and the egg in the pan hit everything around us;
our mother pushed our father away;

she said, I was trying to cook, said, Enough already, then he laughed that laugh, then she was pulling him in, then I had to leave the room;

on our first date, the guy and I went out to dinner;

it was an old-money place in the city;

he watched me chew my food;

he said, I love your mouth;

he had a thing, he said, for a certain mouth;

because his father, he said, had a thing for a certain mouth;

a certain mouth, said his father, was what you wanted;

I said, What does it mean, this certain mouth;

he said, What do you mean what does it mean;

he moved his chair closer to the table;

it was dark, and there was music;

the music was manipulative;

the drinks on the table were manipulative;

then there were more drinks on the table;

when he said, Let's go, we went;

one might call this an obligation;

I might call it a disappointment;

I should call myself that disappointment;

me in the role of idealized me;

me as this girl we all want to fuck;

and were I not just a body like anyone else;

were I not just the parts of a body;

were I not just the parts of the parts;

there was a night I'd been out until late;

we looked at the guy until he looked back, and that was it;

when I got to the house later on, our father was at the door;

he was just getting in from a night, as well;

so it was like we had a secret;

we walked into the house together;

we went into our separate rooms;

I imagine both of us slept;

the next morning, we sat at the table;

it was me and my brother and our father;

our mother was at the stove;

a lot of time passed, us sitting there, waiting to be fed;

and in that time I must have thought something, but I
couldn't tell you what it was;

then our father said, Where were you last night;

and I said, Out with a friend;

and our father said, I said where;

he said, I didn't say with whom;

now food was on the table;

my brother was chewing too hard;

I couldn't stand the sounds he made;

and the sounds at the stove I couldn't stand;

our mother's always annoying sounds;

our mother frying something loudly;

our father said, Where were you last night;

and I said, Where were you;

how can I even convey the tension in that room;

me and our father staring each other down;

my brother chewing harder;

the sounds at the stove even louder;

our father standing, then me standing;

our mother saying, Enough already;

our father looking at our mother;

that animal look on his face;

that look I can't describe;

just I'd seen it someplace else;

like on an actual animal once;

so everything went to shit;

I went after our father with both hands;

and our father went after me;

he was stronger and I knew better;

but once I started really fighting, I got totally carried away;

and once he started really fighting;

when I imagine that scene today, I imagine hair flying;

I imagine dust, then dust settling in an empty room;

but it was just my brother screaming, our mother screaming, the dog jumping up on everything he could;

it was no one knowing where to look;

it was me becoming the girl I would be for the rest of my life;

my head not even in the room;

I was orbiting the stars;

ducking everything coming toward me;

our father coming toward me;

his big hands right up in my face;

but the dog was being way too wild;

when our father kicked it, it made a sound I hear, still, to
this day;

then everyone went to their rooms;

later that night, our father played the piano;

he'd memorized several songs;

none of the songs were good songs;

all of the songs were old and dumb;

sometimes he sang along to them;

sometimes he sang more than one part;

our father had no talent for singing;

he had no talent for playing the piano;

it was only a performance of talent;

but so much talent is actually only that;
on our last night together, the guy said, Baby;
but I wasn't going to look at him;
that night, I decided to look at the portrait;
at that confident guy in his confident suit;
that confident guy staring down at me;
that confident guy getting his way;
pushing my body into a stove;
the cold of the counter against my skin;
a skillet flying across the room;
no one knowing where to look, then looking away, then
looking on;
this is a personal history of not knowing what to feel;
no, this is a universal history of not knowing a fucking
thing;
it turned out my brother did cut his hair;
he was expecting a portrait would be made;
he was disappointed when it was not;
but our father was on his way out by then;
he'd been overthrown by then;
we would be forced to find replacements for our tyrant;
the easiest thing we would ever do;
when the guy fell asleep, I stared at his back;
I listened to the sounds he made;
the room was getting lighter;
at some point, I stood on the bed;
I took the portrait down from the wall;
it was large, and it was heavy;
I had no plan to do anything with it;
I just wanted to look at it closer;
I wanted to see why it mattered;

or I'm lying to you because I don't really know why I did
what I did;
    but the guy woke up and saw me standing;
    I admit I must have looked crazy;
    and it got fucking weird after that;
    I mean imagine what he screamed at me;
    and imagine what I screamed;
    and did he watch my mouth as the words came out;
    that certain mouth he loved;
    a mouth that could do things others could not;
    don't make me regret telling you this;
    don't make me describe my mouth;
    there are pictures of me, if you're curious;
    you can find them, if you want;
    you can zoom right in on my lips;
    you can imagine pressing yours to mine;
    you can imagine how soft mine would be;
    try to imagine how soft things could be;
    then imagine how hard things could be;
    I can make things incredibly hard;

Ghosts

The locals called us things so dumb. Stick-on, they said, when we walked past. They made gestures to represent sticking us on. The gestures involved their hands. They involved their hips moving around. Sometimes they tried to touch our arms. Sometimes, depending on how they looked, we let them almost touch us.

The one we liked worked at the haunted house. He never tried to talk to us. He barely looked at us. One night we said, Can we go in. Not that we even wanted to. We were mostly just fucking around. But he said to go in any time. He would let us in for free, he said. This made us laugh. As if we couldn't afford it, we said. As if our fathers didn't own the whole shore.

My mother and I, at the end of the summer, drank on the terrace in the early evenings. It was our thing we did, drinking and looking at the sky. Some evenings, we listened to loons. Some, we sat in silence. And on one of the evenings, the one I remember more than the others, my mother made one of her jokes. Her jokes weren't proper jokes. They were more like jabs directed at people she didn't like. Like the person she was maddest at at the time. She was maddest, that evening, at my father. So her joke was directed, I remember, at him.

The sound of loons was a sound you couldn't compare to anything else. Though many each summer tried. Many compared the loon sound to a train sound, which it was not. Many compared the loon sound to a human sound, which it also was not. My father said the loon sound was much like the sound of a woman screaming. But when, I thought, had he heard a woman scream like that. And where had he heard that woman scream.

One night, we told the guy to let us in for free. We thought we were being clever with our joke. But the guy didn't get it, or he didn't care. He said, Go in, so we went. It was darker inside than we thought it would be. And colder than we thought it would be. And there were sounds inside. Like howling wolves. Like a storm that sounded nothing like a storm. We held each other's hands at first. Then we touched the things we weren't supposed to touch as we walked past. Like spiderwebs. And body parts. Then the doors opened up to outside. And we were standing there at the rides again, like was that supposed to scare us.

The woman was leaning into my father. She was drinking champagne and leaning in a way that made her look like a doll. This was at a party at the boathouse. The girl and I were standing around being bored. We'd taken the girl's mother's pills. We were waiting for something to happen. Like for the pills to kick in. Like for this woman leaning into my father to fall.

I couldn't remember my mother's joke if I tried. I only remember that it was mean. And that I had to fake a kind of laugh. And that my mother was laughing harder than I was. And it could have meant something, had anyone seen the two of us laughing like that. But then my mother stopped laughing and leaned toward me. She wasn't one to get that close. But she leaned even closer, her face right in front of my face. She was looking at something near my mouth. Then I felt her fingers on me. I said, Get away. And she said, What's that. She said, Is that a crease.

There was a day I went to the rides alone. The locals called out their shit. Like, Shake that ass. Like, Bring that ass over here. Their hands held on to shapes that were mine. They forced themselves right through them. Like forcing themselves through dreams of me. Or forcing themselves through my ghost. The guy let me walk through the haunted house before it opened for the night. With the lights on, it looked even more fucked up. Like a fucked-up person's home. Some kids had written words on the walls. There was trash on the floors. But you could imagine someone living there. The worst of the local guys. There was a corner behind a curtain. A chain inside a metal bucket. The guy said I could stand in the corner. I could do whatever I wanted. Rattle the chain. Jump out at kids.

My father was whispering into the woman's ear. He was holding on to her arm. The woman was younger than my father. She was wearing a skirt that I, if I cared about dressing up, might have worn. Now she was looking at me and waving. Now she clapped her hands to call to me. But I wasn't a dog you could call like that. I said, I'm not your fucking dog. And the girl and I laughed.

Had my mother been there, she might have laughed too. But had my mother been there, the woman wouldn't have been standing with my father. She would have been looking at him, as she often did, from across the room. She would have been talking loudly, to make him look, to make my mother look. So had my mother been there, instead of sitting alone on the terrace, the night might have gone a different way. Had my mother been there, beside my father, imagine.

Under the harshest light I knew, the light in a washroom at the boathouse, I often looked in the mirror. I looked at the different colors in my eyes. I looked as the veins in my temple throbbed and wondered if they were supposed to. But I never saw, under that harshest light, anything even vaguely resembling a crease. I swatted at my mother's hand. She leaned back in her chair. She said, Do you think you won't get old. She said, Do you think you can just freeze time.

You can tell yourself you have control. You can fool yourself for a second. For a fraction of that second. It's some night you feel everlasting. You and your friends are superhuman. Even your dreams that night are of running barefoot through grass.

I stood behind the curtain, holding the chain. When kids walked past, I didn't breathe. It was all about the timing. I wanted to make them feel they were almost to the end. That they were almost to the doors that opened to the rides. And I could have let them get to the doors, get on with the rest of the night. It was good enough just to stand there. To be alone all night in the dark. But I crashed the chain to the bucket. The crash was louder than you would think. And the kids screamed every time. They screamed like you can't even fucking believe.

The woman was clapping her hands to call me over. I wanted to get on my knees. I wanted to crawl to her like a dog might. Even bark at her, I was that fucked up. The girl just would have loved it. We would have joked about it for years. But before I could get on the floor, the woman was walking away. Because my father was walking away. The girl said, Where are they going. She said, Are they going to fuck. Then she was laughing again. So this was something now. So I, without knowing I would be, now, was walking.

I stood in front of my mother and said I didn't think I would get old. I did, in fact, plan to freeze time. So that I will stay young, I said. And so you, I said, will stay old.

The loons didn't sound like a woman screaming. I should have said to my father, You don't even know. You've never heard a woman scream, I should have said. That's a different sound, the sound we make. That's a totally different sound, I should have said. Listen to this, I should have said. Listen to this awful sound we make.

Before the rides closed, some guys came through. They were drunk and loud and came through the way we'd come through that night like what the fuck is this place. They were pounding on the walls and kicking at the walls. And was I scared of them. I was sad for them. I was sad for so many guys. I was sad for the rich guys. Sad for the locals. Sad, at times, for my father. Because they would never get what they wanted. Or they would get what they wanted, but still want more. Then still want even more.

So I decided not to crash the chain. It was the first time I would just let something go. And the guys would leave. And the rides would close. I would walk to the boathouse. I would find the girl. I would tell her how I spent the night. I would make her die in every way. Or I would keep it to myself.

I followed my father and the woman through the boathouse. I followed them into a sitting room. Then they went into a washroom and closed the door. The sitting room had a nautical theme. Much of the shore was nautically themed. Much of our lives was normalized in this way. It made us feel like a club for normal people. I sat on a nautical couch. I knew I didn't have to stay there. I didn't have to do any-thing. My father was in a washroom with a woman. My mother was drinking herself to sleep. And God, I mean where was he. I mean all I can say is the rules had changed and no one was in charge. But someone was going to pay. And someone was going to hell. And I could end the story, here, if I wanted, with this revelation.

The sun was setting, and my mother said, Move. She wanted to see the sunset, she said. I was blocking it with my head, she said. So I blocked it more. I watched my shadow move across my mother's face.

You can lie and say you're in control. Then the awful truth rushes in. You're not at all everlasting. You'll never be super-human. You can't stop things. You can't freeze time. You're in every way like everyone else. Like everything else. You'll end.

The guys didn't leave right away. They kept kicking at the walls. They were saying the drunkest shit. Then one of them pushed at the curtain. Then another one was push-ing. I could feel each push and hard. I mean my body was right fucking there. So now was I scared. I'll tell you what I thought. I thought, just open the curtain. Before they hurt you, I thought. Or kill you, I thought. So I opened it. And they jumped for a second. But then they were laugh-ing. Then they were moving toward me.

I mean they were guys, and I was this. I mean I didn't think I would win. I mean guys fucked the air when I walked past. And what is the word for fucking the thing stand-ing in for a thing.

I don't remember getting up from the sitting room couch. But there I was standing at the washroom door. There I was pushing open the door. The washroom, too, had a nautical theme. Even the sink was nautical. Even the soaps were shell-shaped, even the dish they were in. I saw them before they saw me. I saw the way they were standing. I saw the changing shape of the space between them. And the light changing in that space. The woman tilting like a doll. The woman's hand on my father's shirt. The woman's shirt in the sink.

And as I fell to the washroom floor, it was like everything around me stopped. Then everything was moving again. Was that time freezing, I wonder now. The split second of nothing before pain. Then I felt my father's arms as if through clouds. I felt his shirt against my face. I heard the woman laughing way too hard. I saw her putting on her shirt. Someone's had too much champagne, she said. But I hadn't had champagne. I had taken the girl's mother's pill. And the pill had made me powerful. I was powerful and standing now. So I pushed her into that shell-shaped sink. So I felt how soft her shirt was. I could feel her body through the shirt. Just another girl's body. Like my own warm body. So I stayed on her body. I kept my hands on her body. And fuck her body. Fuck the heat of her body. Fuck the look on her face. The look on my father's.

After the sunset, my mother fell asleep on the terrace. There was one star low in the sky. It was sitting on top of my mother's head. It was sitting there like a crown or something. Like the top of a crown. I'm not sure why I'm telling you this. It was only sad, the star eventually disappearing.

There was a night I stood in the washroom. I stretched open my mouth as wide as I could. I twisted and untwisted the skin around it. And I saw, under that harsh light, that yes there was a very thin crease that would no doubt become—my mother knew this from watching her own face cave—deep and irreversible.

The guys were trying to scare me. But I knew they weren't going to kill me. I mean I was the one holding a chain. And I felt like something as I lifted it up. I don't know what I felt like. Like a guy perhaps. Or a ghost perhaps. And I felt it more as I shook the chain. And I felt it more as I swung it. And my fucking face. I could feel how crazy I'd become. So who was scared now. So who now was running fast through the dark like little girls.

At some point, the lights came on. The wolves shut down. The storm shut down. The guy came in to get me. We stood out front and smoked. Some girls walked shoeless on the dirt. A woman picked up trash with a stick. The rides froze in place all around us.

The sound of loons wasn't the sound, I should have said, of anything but the sound of loons.

The sound of loons wasn't a thing, I should have said, that you'll ever in your life understand.

The sound of a woman screaming, I should have said. I should have screamed.

The locals tried to touch our legs. And what if we let them touch us. What if we bent over for them. What if we shook our asses the way they asked us so many times to shake our asses.

Would they have lifted us up. Would they have stuck us on. Would they have gotten off. Would we have gotten off.

Because we weren't their fucking girls you know. We would never be their fucking girls. We were dreams of girls. We were ghosts of girls. We were dogs.

Liars

were we to get more scientific;
were we to consider the weight of the body;
were we to consider the height from which it fell;
and the temperature of the water;
the position of the moon;
were we to measure the alcohol in the body;
and were there pills in the body;
were there hands on the body;
Don't be crazy, they say;
Don't be like that, they say;
were we to dust the dock for prints;
were we to dust her skin for traces of hair, for traces of
other skin;
were we to trust my older brother;

were we to trust his asshole friends;

and our tyrant fathers;

and our weakass mothers;

and all the younger girls;

were we not this tight-knit group;

were we not this pleased with our fancy selves;

and our circular drives and our heavy gates;

and our terraces and our lawns;

but we're only performing tight-knit group;

our souls despise each other's souls;

and we don't even believe in souls;

but were our fathers kind, our mothers kind;

were the neighbors kind and their asshole kids;

were we not always standing on the dock in the spot where
she last was;

were we not always standing in that spot to understand that
night;

or to understand the girl who drowned;

to feel everything she felt;

our mothers say, Stay away from the dock;

they think they still can save us;

but the body shapes I see in the water;

and the ghost sounds I hear at night;

and the stories they all tell over drinks;

everyone saying she was trashed;

everyone saying she slipped and fell;

You know how she was, they say, as if a person ever can
know;

then the power of the word *was*;

and the subtext before we know the word *subtext*;

and a look before we know how to read those looks we'll
see again and again;

our mothers shaking their heads and saying, What a waste;

our fathers, at times, with nothing to say, at times, with too
much to say;

then it's, That knockout in her underwear;

it's, That knockout out of her crazy head;

That knockout sinking like a stone;

And that's what happens when you drink, they say;

And that's what happens when you fool around;

and when you walk like that;

and when you look like that;

when you look good enough;

when you look good enough to what;

there are nights we watch my brother and his friends on
the dock from up in the trees;

after they leave, we sit on the dock and stare out across the
water;

one night, we waited for the sunrise;

not for any reason other than we were up and it was next;

when she appeared, that night, we jumped;

she was standing all crooked, holding her shoes;

she was looking for her friends, she said;

and had we seen her friends, she said;

you're thinking ghost, but this was before all that;

it was the real her coming from somewhere;

and who knows what she'd been up to;

what asshole guy she'd been with;

perhaps my brother's friend;

we used to like him too;

we used to fuck him all the time;
but we're done with him now;
we're done with them all;
and they'll pay so big someday;
they'll wake someday with guilt around them like a cage;
and they'll remember the details of that night;
and the details of her face;
and the words she said before she fell;
but there's no point in building her character here;
no point in building the perfect girl you always want;
so here's any girl holding her shoes;
any girl looking like some kind of ghost;
any girl pointing to the sky;
like your sister saying, Look at the colors;
your sister saying, Look at that;
we didn't look long at the colors;
we knew what the colors meant;
we knew about light and waves;
so we just looked at her body;
like anyone would have done;
and it could have been us, then, holding our shoes;
it could have been us, nights later;
and do you think we would have been pushed in too;
do you think we would have been held in too;
do you think we would have been flailing too and thinking stop, and thinking you guys, you motherfuckers, then not;
do you think we would have felt that point at which you
just give up;
you stop performing for guys, for other girls;
you let your hair go bad;
you let your gut go big;

then it's only water and always water;

or do you think we're too good for that;

do you think we're just too smart;

do you think we're just too rich;

we swore we would never be like her;

to our mothers, our fathers, we swore it and meant it, but look;

just look at us pushing against the guys;

look how fucked up, how fucking hot;

so imagine a day they'll stand in a spot on the dock where we last were;

they'll shake their heads, say things about us like what a fucking waste;

when we ask for details about that night;

when they catch us listening at the doors;

Get lost, they say;

Don't spy, they say;

It's not spying, we say;

it's a full-on investigation;

we're conducting experiments on the dock;

we like to see how long we can stand on the edge;

we like to see how hard we hit the water when we fall;

we prefer to fall in backward;

to watch the sky move farther away;

to brace ourselves for cold;

to feel the slap against our backs;

to time how long we can stay underneath;

we sometimes hold each other under;

we've learned to kick away;

we've learned to swim to under the dock;

we press our mouths to between the slats and breathe;

this is only about survival;
about how to survive when it's us going in;
about how to save our sorry selves;
so we need to know the exact time of;
the temperature of;
the velocity of;
the height from which;
the phase of the moon;
the weight of the body;
the weight on the body;
the weight of the water pressing down;
but there's nothing more to say, they say;
You're obsessed, they say;
We're worried, they say;
End of story, they say and tell us to go;
End of story, we hear through the walls;
but there's never an end of story;
there's only the start, a night on the dock;
and all the details we already know;
and x for all we don't;
x for the one who touched her last;
x for the one who pushed;
and for her body now in the water;
for her body held under the water;
for her body filling with water;
for her ghost on the dock on our wildest nights;
for her ghost in our beds forever;
for the scream stuck in your heads;
and for what you're about to tell us;
and don't give us your made-up shit;
your knockout in her underwear;

your knockout with her hair all wild;
your fucked-up girl;
your perfect girl;
there's no such thing as perfect girl;
you need to stop lying to yourselves;
you need to start looking at yourselves;
you absolutely will get old and die;
no, you won't absolutely get old;

Animals

; it's the girl saying, I dare you, into my ear; it's me doing whatever she says; it's always me like some kind of child; it's me like some kind of dog; Jump, she says; How high, I say; so obedient; so weak; it's the pill we split in the washroom; and the world now flat like worlds in cartoons; and the grass sucking down in tiny holes; like a thousand mouths pulling us deeper in; and I would happily go there into the holes, my ears stuffed full of grass and dirt; and how pleasant it might be in the dirt, if nothing slithered through it; how pleasant to hide so deep below the ugly noise of this ugly world; but the woman has left her purse on a table; and the girl has dared me to take the purse; and how fucking high; as high as you fucking can; like this one night at the rides; it was us behind a trailer; it was two pills on her outstretched hand; it was a big pill and a small pill; I didn't know what either pill did; and I remembered, then, a film we saw in school about drugs; it said not to judge a pill by its size; the big pill might look more dangerous; but it could be nothing, like a vitamin; it could make your nails grow long; but the small pill could make you crazy; it could make you try to fly off the roof of your house; that night, I took the small one; I chewed it up to make her laugh; I opened my mouth to make her laugh harder; but then the pill kicked in, and things got rough; and the night changed; and we'll get there; for now, we're standing on the boathouse lawn; we're wearing dresses our mothers bought; we're sinking in heels and wishing we were guys; there are people holding trays of food; it's a party for my father; we're celebrating my father; he's done something impressive; he's often doing these very impressive things; now someone on the other side of the lawn is clinking a glass with a knife; that someone wants to give a speech about my father; so my father now is walking to that side of the lawn; my mother is walking beside him; the woman is walking slowly behind them; the woman is closer to my age than my mother's; I'm the only one, at this point, who knows about the woman; I'm the only one who saw them, on another night, in a washroom; I'm the one who saw the woman's face against my father's face; when I think of her face, I think I shouldn't have seen her teeth; I think I shouldn't have seen her eyes half-closed; I think the word *animal* when I think this; I think the words *piece of shit*; I swore to my father I wouldn't tell my mother what I saw; what my father said I thought I saw; what my father said I didn't see; and he made me swear on my mother's life I wouldn't say one word; but I don't believe in the power of swearing on people's lives; I don't believe anyone is listening when I swear; or I do believe someone is listening; and I believe that someone knows I have no other choice; so there will come a night I'll tell it all; I'll make it a fucking exposé; and it'll ruin my father; it'll ruin my mother; it'll ruin the woman; it'll ruin the windows of our house; and the windows of our cars; and my reputation; my entire future; but tonight is a party for my father; it's a perfect night for a party; the sun is setting behind the boathouse; and I'm more fucked up than I'd meant to be; so I'm creeping across the lawn; I'm sinking in holes and everything seems to be slowing down; everything could come to a stop right now; and what would we even lose; but the girl says, Go, and pushes my back; she says, Fucking go, so I go; she doesn't even know whose purse it is; she never gives a shit whose thing it is; she always just wants the thing itself; she just wants the things inside the thing; but I want the owner of the thing; I want to own the owner in some brutal way; I want to own this woman in that way; so which one of us now is in charge; is it the one who dares the other; or is it the one who dares to do the fucking thing; I can hear applause from the other side of the lawn; my father will act like he doesn't deserve it; my mother will hide behind her dark glasses; the woman will plan a life that will never be her life; and as the applause fades out, and my father starts a speech about himself, we reach the table, and I take the purse, and we're running now to the dock; we're screaming, and what can I say about this; just something about the girls we are; or the girls we have to be; so we're spilling the purse out to the slats; the girl puts on the lipstick; I open the pack of gum; I stuff stick after stick into my mouth; and I feel so crazy doing this; and the girl looks crazy sitting there; and what have we become; just animals; just lower than dogs; and is there anything lower than that; the night at the rides I was too fucked up to walk; but we got on the dumbest ride there was; it was this boat-shaped thing that swung; and there was music playing from somewhere; and there were guys watching from the ground; and when the boat started swinging, I was laughing; but when it went higher, I said, Get me off of this fucking ride; I hadn't realized the power of this machine; that it could swing straight up to ninety degrees; that every time at ninety degrees, I could feel myself slipping out of the seat; that every time, my whole ass lifted straight up out of that seat; there was a metal bar to keep us down; but the space between the metal bar and me was as big as I was; I could have slipped out through that space, and what; in the film we saw in school about drugs, a kid kept saying, I can fly; I was secretly hoping he would try it; I wanted to see him soaring; I hoped to feel that good one day; but not to feel that alone; from up high, you could see the other rides and you could see the whole boardwalk as lights; from up high, you could see people like the nothing specks they were; it was colder up high than down below; and the sounds up high were weird and wrong; and going down you felt your gut, just awful, sinking; I closed my eyes and could still feel everything around me; the girl was touching my arm; I could feel the heat from her hand; it felt like the worst thing in the world; like the very last thing before it all goes dark; then she screamed into my ear, Let go; she screamed, Let go of the bar; she knew I could have died like that; she wanted to bring me as close as she could; so I let go of the bar; so I think I prayed; I mean know I prayed to someone; I mean I was saying something to someone; I mean I was swearing to someone, begging for something, believing in something else; the ride eventually slowed, then stopped; we walked off, and the ground was shaking; all of the air was shaking; it was like finally, and I stood very still; and I waited for something that didn't, that night, come; that didn't, for some time, come; then we walked away like nothing; and the night went on; and the days went on; and now she's lying flat on the dock; and I'm looking down and thinking how much I hate her; I'm thinking how much I hate; I throw the gum wrappers into the water; I throw the lipstick into the water; I throw the purse as hard and as far as I can; I take the wallet and leave the girl lying there, eyes closed, looking dead; walking past the boathouse, I hear the party still going on; by now the woman is frantic; by now she's turning over tables; my mother tells me these details when she gets home; how the woman screamed in the face of every person holding every tray, Where's my fucking purse; how much I wish I'd seen this; and had I seen it, I might have claimed it as my own; I might have clinked a glass and said to the crowd that the plan was my idea; I might have said that I pointed to the purse, that I knew the girl would dare me; and I might have said what I saw that night in the washroom; how she looked at me from over my father's shoulder; and how much she looked like an animal; like the kind you see in the dark; and I might have said how hard she laughed; and don't you love this detail; and don't you love this woman; and don't you love my father; and aren't you impressed that I, of all the people, am now at the center of your world; so listen up; I want to tell you the end is near; I want to tell you to box your things; I want to tell you it's going to hurt; I want to tell my mother, my God; but I'm too fucked up to deal with her now; so I go to my room and close the door; I look through the woman's

wallet; the picture on the ID looks just like the girl; it's the
hair, perhaps; or it's the teeth; so I'll give the ID to the girl;
and the ID will never fail her; she'll storm into the market;
she'll slam her bottles to the counter; she'll take the ID from
her pocket; she'll look straight into the cashier's eyes, get what
she wants;

Ghosts

On rides to the shore, when we were kids, we sang a song.

There were two versions of this song we knew.

There was the version we learned from our father, and there was the version we learned, later, from kids at the shore.

We preferred the version we learned from the kids.

And we tried just once, at the end of a ride, to sing this version we preferred.

We didn't do this to anger our father.

We were confused when our father pulled over.

Cars were swerving around us.

Our mother was screaming her head off.

She was screaming things like, What in the world, and, Have you gone completely mad.

My brother and I were like shut the fuck up.

We said, Shut the fuck up, to our mother.

And after she shut completely up, meaning after she'd given completely up, our father restarted the song the way it was meant, according to him, to be sung, and we sang.

I can't explain why we preferred the version we learned from the kids.

Or why my brother, on a night we were driving around, sang it our father's way.

On that night, for the first time ever, we sang the song to its final line.

Our father wasn't with us that night, and our mother wasn't with us.

It was just us in the car, me and my brother, on this ride around the shore.

There was an object my brother's friends had dared him to get from a house on the other side.

The object was a joke between my brother and his friends.

It had become this joke because my brother had clung to it once when he was too fucked up to do anything else.

So his friends had dared him to get this object and bring it back to the boathouse.

Saying no to a dare wasn't an option.

Saying no meant you weren't a good sport.

My brother prided himself on being a good sport.

But we were all good sports.

Our father always started the song, and my brother and I were expected to sing as loudly as we could.

Our mother never sang, as she despised this song more than any song, and she would beg us to stop singing it, saying we were absolutely killing her ears.

But the more she complained about our singing, and the harder she pressed against her ears, the louder we sang, our father always singing the loudest.

Our father had told us many times that he was a great singer, that he'd sung with a group in college, and he would say, Harmonize, to me and my brother, and though we never knew how, our father would try, would go higher, go lower, and always go louder, so we would go louder too.

But even in our most enthusiastic moments, moments in which our mother threatened, to our delight, to open the door and throw herself from the car, we never got even close to the end of the song.

Because even in these very best moments, we had to stop, always, when our mother would pull on her hair and scream, I've had enough, Enough already, I despise you all.

And though our father was always the one to start singing, and though he loved more than anything to anger our mother, to bring her as close as he could to the brink of explosion, he, too, would say, Enough you kids, I said enough.

The rest of the ride was our father silent, staring at the road.

It was our mother pretending to sleep.

It was us in the back, all wound up, still wanting to sing.

I tried, I admit, alone in my room, to get all the way to the end of the song, but could not.

It wasn't because I was lacking in skill, but, rather, because it wasn't a good song to sing alone.

There was something about singing the song alone that suggested drinking alone in a crowded bar, and a desperation I recognized even then.

And I recognized the desperation as a certain messy desperation I'd seen on faces outside bars I wasn't supposed to be anywhere near.

And I recognized the desperation as an adult desperation, one I wouldn't have to face for years, though I would face it, I knew it, even then, we all faced it.

My brother and our father would go on these walks by the water, that were our father's idea, that were guys-only walks.

Our father used these walks to teach my brother about things that were guys-only things, like for instance girls and ways to manage girls.

Our father would teach my brother that the most effective way to manage girls was just to wear them down.

And though my brother already resented our father, and though I knew in my gut there would come a day on which my brother would convey this resentment, they always came back from their walks laughing, often laughing at me.

I would say, in response to their laughing, What, and they would laugh even harder, and I would say, Stop, and they would just go on and on.

What I felt those days is hard to explain, though I've felt it many times since.

It just takes a certain kind of guy and a certain other kind of guy.

It takes a joke going on and on, and you, the girl, at the center.

When we got to the house with the object on its lawn, there were people drinking outside it.

So we kept on driving around.

There was the moon that we said nothing about, and there were trees that we said nothing about.

And I should tell you about the object on the lawn.

I should tell you it was just an anchor, the dumbest thing you've ever seen.

Because it wasn't an actual anchor, but a replica, made of who knows what, of an anchor.

And my brother had clung to the anchor, that one night, all fucked up, refused to let go, refused to go back to the boat-house unless the anchor went as well.

But the anchor was larger than you think, and it was stuck deep in the dirt.

On one of our trips to the shore, our father ran over a dog.

It was a large dog, and in our father's defense, the dog had been lying already in the road.

It turned out, so we learned from its owner, a woman, that the dog just liked to sleep there.

And had we lived on this road, we would have known this.

Had we lived there, we would have slowed our speed like the people who lived on this road must always have done.

But we didn't live on this road, and we would never have lived on this road.

And on the side where we lived, our dogs slept not in roads but on sprawling lawns.

When my brother stopped the car that night, he didn't, at first, remind me of our father.

He didn't remind me of our father because my brother wasn't stopping the car out of anger.

He wasn't stopping the car to punish us, so I wasn't reminded of our father.

He was stopping the car to be dramatic, to give me one of the wild looks we gave each other in the back of our father's car.

The point of these looks, back then, was just to make each other laugh.

Because the one who laughed first was the one toward whom our father's anger was directed.

Because enough meant enough, when our father said it, and it meant enough with the singing and enough with the talking and enough, it turned out, with any noise at all.

So when one of us laughed at the other's looks, our father just about went mad.

I can see, looking back, that our father thought we were laughing at him.

So I can see this, now, as somewhat cruel, this literal laughing behind our father's back.

But I also can see this cruelty as a cruelty we were forced to inherit from our father.

Like so many things we didn't want but got and still, to this day, have.

But I wasn't reminded of our father as my brother looked at me all wild, stopped there in the road.

I wasn't reminded of our father, but of a younger version of my brother and a younger version of myself.

And I saw these younger versions of ourselves as two people on the same team or in the same camp or whatever metaphor you want.

And it wasn't until my brother started singing our father's version of the song that I was reminded of our father.

And it wasn't until I said, No, and, Stop, and nearly covered my ears that I was reminded of our mother.

But I wasn't our mother, and I would never be our mother.

I was one kind of weak, but I would never be that other kind of weak.

So I sang with my brother, loudly as I could, that fucking song we never liked.

It was a party, that one night, on the other side.

My brother was too fucked up.

I left him lying on the lawn.

I couldn't find my brother's friends.

Inside the house was a smell of mold.

There was a smell of smoke, a smell of beer.

There were plastic tables and plastic chairs.

There were ring-shaped stains on the rug.

A filthy guy was staring at me.

He said, Sit, but I wouldn't sit.

There were pizza boxes on the chairs.

The freezer door was tied shut with a string.

The guy said, You should sit.

I went outside to look for my brother's friends.

They were now on the lawn, throwing my brother's shoe over my brother's head.

When the shoe landed on the roof, his friends said, Let's get his other shoe.

It was then my brother ran to the anchor on the lawn and clung to it how he did.

It's hard to explain his position.

The awkward way his legs were bent.

How tightly he was holding on.

His friends were laughing harder than I'd seen them laugh.

And it was funny at first, but then I said, Just pick him up.

Then I said, Just carry him.

It took a long time, but eventually his friends dragged him away.

And the anchor became another dumb joke they would keep alive forever.

Moments before our father ran over the dog, our mother had cracked.

She was everywhere in that moment, just on everyone in that moment.

She was screaming and she was screaming words she shouldn't have said.

She was pulling her hair and her eyes looked wild.

Because our father was being too much our father.

He was singing too hard that awful song.

He was singing too loudly, and our mother, I swear, opened that door to throw herself from the car.

And were we secretly hoping.

I can only speak for myself.

Now our father was driving way too fast.

Our mother eventually closed the door.

Some kids on the side of the road were waving at our car.

I saw the kids, but our father, I have to believe, did not.

And before I could scream, and I did scream, Stop, and grabbed our father's arm from behind, there was this thump.

At first, I thought our father would keep on driving.

But he stopped the car right there and got out.

The kids were crying and covering their faces.

Their mother ran out of their shitty house, covering her face.

My brother and I got out of the car, and our father said, Get back in the fucking car.

And we did get back in the car.

But first, I saw this hit dog lying in the road and its eye that something was wrong with.

There were still people standing on the lawn, so we kept on driving and we kept on singing louder and harder than we'd ever sung this song.

Sometimes we sang in accents.

Sometimes we fake harmonized.

My brother's face was wild and I'm sure mine was wild as well.

And had you heard us singing, you might have thought we'd gone completely mad.

Or you might have sung along.

You might have better understood us.

But I'm not trying to make this night more special than it was.

I'm not saying we achieved some great thing by singing the song to its final line.

I'm actually saying there was nothing we achieved.

Because we didn't sing to the final word.

Because in the version we sang, our father's version, there was no way to get to the final word.

Because the final line, we realized that day, as we tried to sing it, was flawed.

I mean grammatically and I mean metrically, so we stumbled through it, so we stumbled again, and I was like fuck this song and stopped.

Perhaps needless to say, the final line in our preferred version, the one now going through my head, wasn't flawed.

And had we chosen to sing our preferred version, we would have gotten to the final word.

But here we were, and the details of the line don't matter.

The words themselves, don't think about those.

Just think about what it was to get there, after all those years, and realize.

My brother would start college in the fall.

He would go to the college our father went to.

He would major in the same thing our father did.
He would try to find the singing group our father was in.
But there would be no singing group.
This would be no surprise to me.
To my brother, though, this would be a disappointment.
And there would be many more disappointments.
And, eventually, my brother would go after our father.
No, I was the one who would.

It would start, for me, as a seed, for lack of a better word,
moving into my gut.
On that day, there would be too many seeds, and they would
bloom at roughly the same awful time.
On that day, I would go after our father with both hands.
It wouldn't be the first time I did.
The first time was at the shore.
And I lost that time.
I wasn't ready that time.
But the next time, I would be.
It would be a scene like you can't believe.
Imagine things that shouldn't fly flying.
But that's another story.
And I'll tell that story another time.

Our father told us get back in the car, and we did.
We watched the rest of the scene through the window.
The mother crying, her kids crying.
Our father saying something to the mother.
Our father wearing the mother down.

Because it was her fault, he would say to her, that the dog was sleeping in the road.

And what kind of person, he would say to her, would let a dog just sleep there like that.

We watched the woman's body wilt, her face wilt, the kids' faces almost too sad to look at.

And their poor sad house behind them.

The whole world sad around it.

That evening, our father and my brother took one of their walks.

Our mother locked herself in a room, and I lay on our sprawling lawn.

I was thinking how we owned that lawn.

I was thinking how there was room on that lawn for a thousand dogs and room for a thousand kids.

I could see the sun through my eyelids.

I could feel our orbit of the sun.

There was almost quiet then.

I even dreamed for a second.

It was a dream about water.

Then my brother was making shadows on my face.

Our father, too, was looming above.

They were laughing at me, and I wasn't in the mood.

I wasn't going to play my part.

So I stood and walked across the lawn.

And I didn't come back.

So I'm not a good sport.

So I ruin a joke.
I ruin their lives.

No, I only ruin my brother's.
Because he wants to keep on singing.
He wants to get to the final word.
But I'm looking out the window now.
I'm pushing through the window.
There are trees out here.
The moon right there.
There's no one now on the lawn.
So it's time to stop the car, brother.
It's time to run like wild, brother.
Time to pull that fucking anchor from the dirt.

Killers

There once was a madman who lived beneath my bed. This was when I was younger. This was when things were different. Then I would call out for my father, wait for him to snap on the light, kneel by the bed, assure me there was no one hiding beneath it.

The first time I called out for my father, my father said, Madman. He said, Where did you get that word. But I didn't know, then, where I got the word. It just came to my mind that night in the dark and made me call out for my father.

My mind, I'd been told, was unlike the minds of others. I'd been told since birth I was greater than most. I couldn't remember being told this at birth. I, of course, couldn't remember birth. A gift, I thought, that one couldn't remember the mess.

It was only my father I called for, nights. My mother was too sound a sleeper ever to wake. She's uncivilized, said my father, mornings, when my mother was still asleep. He would sit at the table, waiting to be fed, and called it, too, uncivilized, this waiting.

The coast is clear, my father would say. Those words made me think of sun-scorched men in stiff green pants. Of a quiet beach before a thousand wretched deaths. But I would keep this image to myself. I would lie there, silent, as my father stood, as the light went out, as I watched my father's sleeve shrink in the thinning strip of hallway light as he closed the bedroom door.

But there was no reason now to think a madman was hiding beneath my bed. I was older now, and a madman simply could enter the room, straddle my thighs, stare down at me until I wake. A madman could breathe into my face an awful smell through yellowed teeth. He could whisper softly into my mouth, You're dead.

So perhaps this is why, one night, on a bed, hearing heavy footsteps on the stairs, hearing doors open, hearing them slam, I thought a madman was coming to get me. So I said to the guy I was with, Get up. I said, Go, and pushed him out of the bed and toward the terrace door.

I didn't think then to go with him. How the rest of the night could have been. Both of us climbing down to the lawn. Running across the grass. I only thought to stay where I was. To lie there, looking up. And when the door opened, I closed my eyes. Then I felt the weight. Then felt the heat. The bedsprings pushing into my back.

The night began on the boardwalk. Me and the girl standing at the rides. Pills dissolved in our sodas. We stood there after the rides had closed. Then the ground was pulling like gravity pulling too hard. Like a black hole pulling, and then I was down. Then a summer cop was coming. Then the guy from the haunted house was coming. I could see them in the distance. Fucking saviors coming to fix it all.

My mind, I'd been told, wasn't unlike my father's mind. It wasn't his mind, exactly. Meaning not at the level of his mind. But it wasn't, in several ways, unlike it.

My father said my first word was *star*. That I pointed to the sky, opened my mouth, and out came *star*, of all the words to begin with. He saw it as a sign of some great thing. That I was destined, he said, to be that. But my mother said my first word wasn't *star*, but *stop*. She said my father must have misheard me. My father, she said, was pulling my hair. And one can see, she said, how what I said, which was *stop*, pointing not to the sky, but to my head, might have sounded like *star*.

I told my mother my father's woman had gone completely mad. She was after me, I told my mother, and my mother

said she was not. Because my mother didn't know everything yet. I mean she didn't officially know. And I was
prone, said my mother, to imagining things. That woman
is just a rich bitch, she said. Another rich bitch, she said, at
the shore. The daughter, she said, of yet another rich bitch.

The cop helped me up from the ground. By then, the girl was
gone. Even she called the cops pigs. Even she ran when a
cop was coming. He bent me into sitting on a bench. He
told me to look straight ahead. I don't remember everything. I do remember I said, Fuck you. This wasn't our
first situation, mine and the cop's. And the guy from the
haunted house. He was kneeling, now, in front of my legs.

There was a morning my father was pouting at the table.
When I pouted like that, my father said, I'll wipe that pout
from your face. He said, You're acting like a child. But
I was a child when I pouted like one, so there was a difference between my pout and his because the food wasn't
yet on the table.

When my father's woman walked past me at parties, I whispered, Dumb bitch. I whispered, Dumb cunt. Yes you, I
whispered. She was always at the parties. She was always
dressed like that. Always following my father around like
a pet. Fuck you, I whispered when she walked past. Fuck
you, walking by her family's house. Fucking piece of shit,
as I threw a rock as hard as I could at whatever window.

But I only threw a rock once. So the night really began with
this. Finding the rock in the garden. Not aiming, just

throwing wildly. Then, after a second of nothing, I heard the crash. The girl and I were like fuck, and we ran. It was more than we'd expected. It was like something big was going on. A different kind of trouble. So we ran to the boardwalk and drank our sodas and waited.

I often wondered if others feared, as much as I did, what lay beneath their beds. Or if I was the only one who watched the ceiling lighten, thinking of God, of how little I knew about God.

I often wondered if others thought of an ocean moving backward. An ocean pulling into itself. Then nothing but sand all the way back. A tidal wave building far from the shore. The longest wait.

I moved my leg to touch the guy's leg. I did this by barely moving it. I pretended it was accidental. The cop said he would walk me home. He extended his hand, and I looked at it. The guy said he would walk me. The cop didn't care who did it. I said I wasn't going home. I was going to the boathouse, I said. The cop and the guy looked at each other. Guys did this when you were difficult. But the guy walked me to the boathouse. He held my arm like I was old. We walked so slowly. Like the speed of trees, I almost said. I knew better than to say something dumb as that. When we got to the dock, I wanted to sit there with the guy. I knew every inch of that dock. I knew every house around it. I knew every rich bitch inside every house. I would tell him all I knew. There were stories, and some were scandals. There was our scandal, too, and I could point to her family's house. He said we shouldn't go on the dock. It was late, he said. You should lie down, he said. But I was already feeling better. It was that kind of pill. Like a sudden explosion in your head. Like all the stars exploding at once. Then a black hole pulling. Then nothing.

My father was the one who told me there was no soul. One died then rotted, my father said. Like fruit, he said. And don't expect more than that, he said. My mother always said not to listen to him. Just because he would rot, she said, didn't mean that I would rot. My father said not to listen to her. Of course I would rot, he said.

But I heard that a man died in an airtight box made of glass. That when the man died, the glass shattered. I heard this from the girl who would drown. It was the only night just me and her. It was a night I meant to be alone. I was lying on the dock, looking at the sky. And then she was lying there too. And what was I seeing this time, she said. The same planets as last time, I said. And did I believe in something more, she said. There was nothing more, I said. So next she was talking about this man. She said his soul burst through the glass. And I could believe a man died in a glass box. I could even believe the glass shattered. But only because the body, after death, still can violently move.

I understood why my father would want to wipe a pout from a face. He looked pathetic, pouting like that. I snapped my fingers in front of his eyes. And he looked up at me with his face still in that awful shape. That dumb sad shape.

There were guys on the boathouse lawn. The girl was there now too. I thought, at first, to join them. I would tell the guys I fell. I would tell them the girl ran off. She's a bitch, I would say. Such a bitch, I would say to her face. One of her eyes was bigger than the other. Now would be the time to say it. But I was with the guy from the haunted house. And the girl would have to deal with that. And the guys would have to deal with her. Because here we were walking inside.

I told my mother my father's woman could kill. My mother said she couldn't kill. Your imagination, my mother said. But it wasn't my imagination. My mother didn't see her staring at me, so many nights, from across a room. My mother didn't see her shape her hands like a gun, raise the gun, and shoot me.

And my mother didn't see me throw the rock. She didn't hear the window break. She didn't hear the woman's screams from inside the house. Saying she was coming to get me. Saying she was going to kill me. And not to worry, she would find me.

We went upstairs and into a guest room. The guy said I should lie down. On the ceiling was a shadow in the shape of a dog. It looked like a dog I knew. The guy said he could stay for a while. We can talk, he said. Then let's talk, I said as a joke, like what was this, school. He sat on the edge of the bed. He said we could talk about the weather. Then he said something about the weather. He said he knew the weather was good when he felt nothing. That is to say, he

felt neither hot nor cold. I wanted, at first, to laugh at this.
But I understood what he meant. I told him that was the
kind of weather my mother, before she turned into a bitch,
called delicious. It was then the guy touched my arm. And
I had what felt like a life-changing thought. But soon I
would hear the footsteps. The madman coming to get me.
So the guy would leave. And the thought would too. And
so my life would go on, for this time, unchanged.

I snapped again in front of my father's eyes. He looked up at
me, and I thought he might actually talk. But he grabbed
my fingers and squeezed until I could hear my fingers
cracking. I screamed so hard my mother walked in looking like God don't make me say. She said, What the hell.
My father let go. He left the house.

My mind, I'd been told, was above average. My father's, I'd
been told, was superior. But his mind was not superior. It
turned out to be an inferior mind. Meaning mine must
have been far less than that.

The girl who would drown said they timed how long it took
the soul to burst the glass. It took just seconds, she said,
but I was done. I mean I wanted to believe her. But to believe her, I needed to be her. And to be her, I needed to
be something so far from what I was. So I said, There is
no soul. But your hair will still grow in the grave, I said.
And your nails will still grow in the grave. And your body
will twitch and seem alive. And I wanted to stay there
longer with her. A part of me did, I now can admit. But

I stood and walked away. And the night, like so many, went somewhere else. And the summer went somewhere else.

There was never a madman beneath my bed. But you know this already. The coast was always clear.

So it wasn't a madman coming into the room. No madman on top of me on the bed. No madman's weight pressing into my ribs. The bedsprings pushing into my spine.

So what should we call it. Just madwoman. My father's woman. Her one hand on my chest. The other raised in a fist. Like some kind of climactic moment. Like she was the bad guy, and I was the girl. Like she was out of her mind, saying into my face, You're dead, you're dead, you're dead.

And I thought to scream. I knew I should. I knew the speed of sound. How it traveled through rooms. Through pictures on walls. Through wires in walls. Down stairs, through doors. So I knew the guys would hear me. The girl would hear me too. Then she would have a decision to make. Save me from my father's woman, or be a bitch. I know what I would have done.

But I didn't make a sound. Because as her fist reached my face, I felt like I was floating. I could look down from the ceiling. I could look down at her hair, her dress. At my body sticking out from hers. My body looking like I'd been dropped. My hair like vines on the pillow.

And I now want to ask the girl who drowned was that the soul. Some scared thing that leaves the body when the body needs it most.

Later, my father's woman would lift a heavy chair from our lawn. This would be after my mother officially knew. After everything went to shit. She would hold the chair over her head. Someone would see her do this. Our neighbor out front walking her dog. She would be absolutely terrified. Too terrified to stop my father's woman from throwing the chair through a window.

Later, my mother would say I was right. She could have killed you, she would say. But she didn't, I would say. I lived, I would say.

And I only lived because the sky was turning light. And the boathouse help arrived. I could hear them downstairs moving things around. I could hear them coming upstairs. And did she want them to find us like that.

So all that happened was a transfer of power. My father's woman climbing off the bed. My father's woman running to the terrace, slamming the terrace door.

All that happened was my rib cage falling back into place. The bedsprings creaking upward.

When a line of light came into the room, I watched it move across the floor. I watched it bend around everything. And I thought God. And thinking God made me think God again.

When there was nothing more to say about the weather, we
were quiet. Then he touched my arm down to my hand. His
mouth was at my ear. His hand was in my hair. I looked for
the shadow in the shape of a dog, but the shadow was now
in the shape of something else.

And I thought about the tidal wave. This isn't a metaphor for
bodies. Not for the things that bodies do. I wanted to hear
an actual roar. To be in the shadow as it started its break.
And us just lying there like that. Us just drowning there.

My mother once said, The weather is delicious, and held out
her arms and spun. I must have been about four then. I
must have been ecstatic when I was four, not knowing that
each thing that touched me would leave its mark.

The story starts with a thing you'll never remember. Then
a wide-open mind. Then words as something other than
words. Then everything else. The same story for us all.

The story starts with a body rising. A door slammed hard.
Pictures shaking on the walls. The heavy picture above the
bed. This heavy picture coming loose, now coming down.

The story ends with brace yourself. It ends brace yourself for
pain. But it's all for nothing. You've been saved again. The
picture just dangles from a wire. Some dumb waste of a
miracle.

Saviors

This is a story about context. About things being out of context.

There's no closer read to do than that.

Starting with my brother being out of context. A night my brother is on a dare. It's a nightly thing, this kind of dare.

Get in a stranger's car, they say.

Or, Get in a stranger's car, they say, and drive.

Parts of my brother's brain, these days, don't connect with other parts of his brain. It has something to do with synapses, something to do with neurons.

Think of it as short-circuiting. Fried wiring.

Think fork in the socket. Blow dryer in the bathtub.

Or just think the pills he takes that are our mother's pills for something. They're in a drawer by our mother's side of the bed. Our mother has said to us both, more than once, Don't ever touch this drawer.

But my brother is getting into everything that isn't his. Like other people's cars, and now our mother's drawer that our mother specifically said not to touch.

The market is always open. The locals are the ones who shop there. We only shop there when we're desperate and it's late. When we're out of something absolutely essential.

The cars outside the market are often unlocked. Sometimes the cars are running. The locals make it too easy for my brother. He gets into the cars like he owns them. It's a whole big show, my brother getting into the cars. And his friends just laugh, all fucked up, across the street.

My brother will only drive a car away once. That night, he'll be missing for hours, and my brother's friends will all pretend they aren't worried. They'll make it into a joke how they often do with things that make them feel.

He's probably in another state, they'll say.

He's probably picked up a girl, they'll say.

But they'll drive around looking, all night, for my brother.

The cop will drive around all night.

He'll tell me to wait at the boathouse.

In case he goes there, he'll say.

So I'll wait on the boathouse lawn for my brother who I know will never show up.

On all of the other nights, my brother just stays in the lot. The locals come out of the market, see my brother sitting in their cars. They tap on the windows. Some of them pound their fists. Some of them open the doors and try to reason with my brother.

But most just stand away from the car, too confused by my brother to do a thing.

And it doesn't matter what they do, besides. My brother won't get out of their cars. The owners have to call for help. And when the cop comes, my brother's friends, assholes that they are, run.

This time, the owner is a woman. She's standing by a wall, holding a bag of groceries. My brother is in the passenger's seat. The cop is standing by the driver's side.

Some nights, the cop has to approach the car slowly. He has to make sure my brother isn't wild. Some nights, he's too worked up. Some nights, he takes swings at the cop. One night, he broke a windshield.

Some nights, he says things that make no sense. Like the time he spoke a series of numbers. The cop was like, what was that.

Some nights, my brother is passed out cold on the seat. On these nights, the cop has to call for backup, then other cops stand there, radios hissing on their shirts.

On these nights, the cop says I should go home. They can take it from there, he says.

On this night, though, my brother is awake. He's looking at the cop through the window. He makes his fingers into a gun. He points his gun at the cop. He points it at the cop's gun.

I hadn't noticed, before this, the cop's gun. I'm sure the cop doesn't use it. Because he isn't a real cop, but a summer cop. He looks too young to be a real cop. He isn't a cop who shoots at things.

When the phone rings, nights, our mother ignores it. My brother and his friends have turned, this summer, our mother says, into trouble.

My brother is pushing it, our mother says.

He is treading, she says, on thin ice.

But my brother is just fucked up in the way that most of us are this summer. The difference is he's learned how not to care. Or he's learned how not to feel.

Blame our mother's pills or blame some skill not all of us have. But our mother has reached her limit. She's at her absolute edge.

So I'm the one who answers the phone each time it rings. I'm the one who helps the cop with my brother sitting in some stranger's car.

I've been spending time, alone, in our father's study. Our father's study smells like apple tobacco, which doesn't smell like apples.

I was once attracted to the picture of the apple on the bag. So I once tried to eat pieces of tobacco when our father was putting it into his pipe.

Our father said, Go ahead.
He said, It won't hurt you.
The tobacco tasted like dirt.
Our father said, Go ahead.
He said, It won't kill you.

The woman who owns the car is a local. You can tell this by her car. And by what she's wearing. And how she's standing against the wall.

She says, Get him out.

The cop says, Calm down.

She says, I will not calm down.

She hugs her bag and looks at her car, at my brother sitting inside it. But looking at him like that won't break him down. He's been known to sit for a very long time. And the cop has been known to stand there, useless, for just as long.

The night before our father left, he grabbed our mother's wrist as she was walking through a room. To talk, he said, but our mother said she had nothing to say and tried to pull away from our father.

Our father seemed to forget where we were. Not physically. But more in terms of schedule.

He seemed to forget he was scheduled to leave us the following day. That he was leaving us to be with his woman. That we were in the process of adjusting to his leaving.

. . .

My brother's friends will find the car my brother took stuck in sand by the water. They'll find my brother inside the car, his head pressed to the wheel.

At first, it'll look to his friends like my brother is sleeping. They'll make some jokes like wake that lazy fucker up. And they'll go on like this, as they often do, for as long as they can.

The cop knocks on the window. He has one hand on his nightstick.

I'm scared, I admit, of what might happen. Bad things have happened, and the cop, too, is likely scared.

My brother presses his face to the window.

He says, Call my fucking mother.

He says, Call my fucking sister.

We have your sister, the cop says.

He says, This is your sister right here.

The cop shakes his head and looks at me. He laughs and wants me to laugh as well. He wants this to be our private joke. My fucked-up brother not seeing that I'm right here.

But the cop isn't even a real cop. So I'm not going to have a joke with him.

Instead I tell him to get my brother out of the car. It's his job, I say, to get my brother out. Or I'll call our father, I say.

The cop doesn't want me calling our father. Even the locals know what our father is like.

Not that our father is even around. I mean now that he's gone. But the cop doesn't know our lives.

. . .

The girl once dared me to steal from the market. The thing I stole had to be longer than my arm.

It was a dumb dare. There weren't many things that long in the market.

There was beef jerky nearly as long as my arm. And there were watermelons nearly that long.

I walked the aisles and found a statue of something holy. It was a statue of a person. I can't even tell you who it was. And I didn't know if it was for sale. But I walked right out, carrying the statue like it was mine.

I, too, have looked in our mother's drawer. I've held the bottle of pills. I've shaken it. I've opened it and looked inside.

I've thought about taking the pills. And I'll take the pills in the near future. Just to see if they do the same things to me. Make my brain fire all wild. Make me some broken-down machine.

Most nights, I walk my brother back to the house. He often wants to stop somewhere to eat. The only place open, besides the market, is on the boardwalk.

Then it's terrible having to sit with my brother. Terrible how fast he eats.

How I have to say, Slow down.

I have to say, It's not going to run off your plate.

In our father's study, I sit in his leather chair. I put my feet up on the desk. I put my feet up on the other leather chair.

In my head, I tell our father's woman, Sit here.
In my head, I tell her, Do this.
I can't tell you what this is about.
It's something to do with power. I mean my lack of power.
There are ways I want to hurt her.
There are many ways, I now can admit.
I won't hurt you, I tell her, in my head.

Our mother was kicking our father's legs. It was pathetic
how weak our mother was. How persistent our father was.

He said, Kids, go to your rooms.

But we were too old to send to our rooms. So we stood right
there and waited for our mother to win.

My brother's friends will think my brother is sleeping in
the car. But my brother's arms won't be how sleeping people
often hold their arms.

They'll then have a decision to make. To take this seriously
or not.

They'll decide to take this seriously.

They'll try to open the doors. But the doors will be locked.
The windows will be up. So they'll bang on the windows.
They'll push on the body of the car.

When our father brought me into his study, it meant I was
in trouble.

Like when I stole the statue from the market. The cashier
dragged me back inside. He called our father and stared me

down. Our father was enraged. Not enraged at me, but at the cashier for calling when our father was working.

Then, later, at home, it was me he was enraged with. Then he yelled at me for stealing. He said stealing was for the poor. And did I want people thinking I was poor.

I walked in on them, and the woman saw me walk in.

I've told this story a thousand times. I've told it a million fucking times.

That I saw them and she saw me. That she didn't let go of our father. That she looked at me while touching him like what are you going to do.

Like he's not your father now.

She said something into our father's ear.

There was a lot happening in a little time.

And I knew one of us in that room was to blame. Not just for that moment, but for all the moments that happened before and all that would happen after.

My brother punches the windshield, and the woman drops her bag.

I can see what sad groceries she's bought. I can see she's a desperate woman, and she's moving, now, toward her car.

This isn't a good idea. The cop and I know what my brother is capable of. Bad things have happened many times. So the cop tells the woman to stay where she is. He'll take care of this, he says.

But the woman says she's done. She's fed up, she says, with this dumb game. She wants to go home, she says.

And I wonder for a second about her home, what's even there.

Our mother never pulled away from our father. It was my brother who disconnected them. He yanked them apart with a force that surprised us all.

Then he left the house and didn't come back for the night.

Our mother went to a guest room and slammed the door, then opened the door, then slammed it.

Our father just stood there, staring at a wall. I felt sorry for him in that moment, and then I didn't. And I didn't for a very long time.

But I will in the future, when he loses it all. I mean the near future. And I mean it all.

There are nights when my brother's brain is firing correctly. On these nights, he's more like he used to be.

On these nights, my brother says the other nights, the rougher nights, will make for a good story. Like someday they'll be funny to us.

Like the night he thought he was stuck on a lawn.

Like the night he let the dog fall from the window.

But it wasn't a good story, as it turned out, my brother just being a lazy fucker on a lawn.

And it wasn't a good story, the dog with three legs bandaged up.

Then all the nights him acting up in strangers' cars.

Then the car he drove away in. The car stuck in the sand. My brother inside, his head to the wheel.

Then one of his friends smashing a window. One of them running to the boathouse. One of them calling for help.

The cop standing by the car that day won't say, Good story.

But my brother won't be dead that day. He'll just be passed out like a dumb bitch. Just passed out cold at the wheel.

One night, we were eating dinner, and our mother left the room.

Then she came back holding a shirt and said, What's this.

Our father, not looking up, said, What's what.

And our mother said, This, and held the shirt high, and our father looked up and said, What.

Our mother said, This, and our father sighed and looked at me and said, It looks like a shirt, and ate.

Our mother stretched out the shirt, which was a woman's shirt, and said, Whose shirt is this, and our father said, Is it yours.

Our mother said, No it's not mine, and our father said to me, Is it yours, and I said, No.

So our father said to my brother, Is it yours, and my brother looked at his plate, and our father laughed and said, I guess we have a mystery on our hands.

And our mother said, I guess we have a mystery on *your* hands, and she threw the shirt at our father, and it made a painful-sounding smack, and it fell into his food, and our father looked at us, and the phone was ringing, and our mother, again, left the room.

Now my brother punches the windshield harder. He punches with the force that's needed to crack it. We know the force that's needed.

The cop is reaching for his radio. There's static, then the cop talking numbers into his shirt.

The woman is walking through the lot. She's walking straight to her car. Her face looks fierce, and this will be something. This will be a whole big show.

Our father had brought me into his study. He told me to sit. Neither of us talked at first.

I could hear sounds from another room. Music or dishes. It doesn't matter.

What you saw, he said.

What you think you saw, he said.

And I remembered a dream I had the night before. In the dream, I was standing in a field. And I was able to see the back of my head, while seeing through the front of my head.

And remembering the dream wasn't unlike having the dream.

I mean I was part there, part not.

Our father looked at me too hard. The study smelled like tobacco. And it wasn't even good for you. I'm not sure why he ever let me eat it.

What you think you saw, he said.

He said, You didn't see.

Then he held out his hand to shake mine.
We were making some kind of deal.
You can't say a word, he said.
You need to swear, he said.
On your mother's life, he said.
As if he even believed in the power of swearing.
I was at the point where I almost believed.
I mean I wanted so much to believe.
So I swore on our mother's life.
So I swore on our father's life.
Because fuck them both for putting me there.
So I was going to hell.

I told our mother after she found the shirt.
How I pushed the woman into the sink.
How I held her there like what are you going to do.
I mean I thought our mother would want to know.
I mean everyone wanted to know.
But the way our mother was looking at me.
Like I'd become some brutal guy.
Like I was now that fucking guy.

By the time I get to the car that night, my brother will be gone. One of his friends will have walked him home.

It'll just be the cop standing by the car. And it won't be night but light already. The following day already.

We'll both look at the water.

I'll be tempted to talk about it.

Say something about how still it is.

Or something about how blue it is.
But the cop will say, He's going to kill himself.
He'll say, Is that what you want.
I'll say, Is that what you want.
He'll say, Is that what you want.

The statue was big, and it was heavy, and it must have been important.

I meant to take it all the way to the boathouse. I meant to hold it high above my head. I would hold it like the holy thing I knew it was standing in for.

And the girl would just die laughing. Everyone would just die. Because what a fucked-up thing, of all the things, to steal.

But they would never know the feeling I had standing outside the market. The feeling of power that came from stealing.

Or it came from the thing I stole.

Or it came from feeling like part of a club.

It came from our father, and I mean *Our father, who.*

For a second it felt holy.

And in the next second, I was stopped.

And had I not been caught, it might have been something that changed my life for good.

Now my brother is punching the windshield with both fists.

In another context, this could be funny, his arms just firing, wild.

In that other context, this could be one of those stories we tell for years.

But there's nothing funny, in this moment, about my brother.

And there's nothing funny about the cop.

There's nothing funny at all about this night like any fucking night.

No, there's something funny about the woman.

It's the way she's running to her car.

The way her shoes land hard on the ground.

And the insects crashing into her face.

And her poor windshield about to crack.

And the cop saying, Stop, like she's going to stop.

The cop saying, I said stop, and what.

I mean what's the cop even going to do.

Do you think he's going to chase her down.

Do you think he's going to shoot her.

Stars

if I call this story the one true one;
say there's something I have to say;
say the many ways of saying it;
say the many ways of not;
like starting somewhere in the faraway past;
because everything starts at the same dumb point;
the void, the big bang, the expansion into;
the world we know or say we know;
I'll say summer, then, at the shore;
say our house was the biggest house there;
say my father was gone, and my mother was such a bitch;
say we went to the jetty, now, to get fucked up;
because the jetty was higher than the dock;
the water was rougher below;

and the local guys who followed us there;

the guy I liked, and the game the girl and I played;

it should never have been a game;

it was all about scaring ourselves;

we were addicted to being scared;

we wanted so much that feeling of something coming to get us;

we wanted that something to whisper into our mouths, You're fucking done;

this had to do with our privilege;

with our private schools in the city;

and being groomed to be something big;

I was being groomed to take over;

and I mean the world, and I mean it all;

but my mother decided to punish me;

because I'd fucked up is the reason she gave;

so she pulled me out of private school;

To build your character, she said;

Your character, she said, is weak;

because I'd gotten too good at our game;

it had become such a competition;

it had become a sort of fixation;

it was something to do with the girl;

I was done with her;

so I wanted to be the best at it, and I was;

I practiced in my bedroom, standing on the edge of my bed;

I pretended the floor was the water;

I pretended the things inside it;

such murderous things, and you sometimes had to take that risk;

even balanced on one leg;

even on your weak leg;

even when your mother walked into the room, said, What in the hell;

and then, at night, on the actual jetty, the real water crazy below;

we lured so many guys there on that one night;

we said we had beer, we would play our game;

the guys could watch us standing on the edge;

like stuck in some kind of system;

like binary stars, some tragic orbit;

waiting for a force to reroute us;

the very definition of game;

not brutal, though, like the games the guys played;

like the one they called buried in the sand;

the one they called dart in your face;

they watched us until they got bored;

and you never got used to their boredom;

you tried anything to lure them back;

you did any dumb thing to make them watch;

take another day that summer;

a basketball hoop on the other side;

the local guys splitting into teams;

us girls on the grass like where are you going;

so we decided we would play too;

neither of us had basketball skills;

we didn't care about being good out there;

we just cared about looking good;

but the game just didn't end well;

I mean it didn't end well for me;

because I broke two fingers in the game;

because the girl blocked me as I was shooting;

and being stopped midshot: this is what I mean by force;
and falling to the ground: this is what I mean by rerouting;
and when the guy I liked ran over;
the only one who was moving;
not even the girl was moving;
and the girl had ruined the whole fucking game;
no, I ruined the game by competing;
I'd been known to compete, to ruin it all;
now this is my mother's voice;
this is me getting scolded;
this is another day, the morning after the night on the jetty,
everyone still crazy;
but it wasn't my fault, I said;
it was the girl's own fault, I said;
I was already done with the game;
and that's true in a way;
I mean the beer was gone, and the guys were bored;
so I was done with the game, but I deep down also wanted
to win;
this is the definition of privilege;
to think you can have it both ways;
and to think you can;
well, you fucking can't;
when I screamed, it was just to speed up the game;
it was just to get attention;
I screamed, I'm taking off my shirt;
I wasn't taking off my shirt;
but now the guys were watching again;
and the girl was laughing at what I said;
I guess I knew she would laugh;
but I didn't think she would fall;

because no one ever, before this night, did;
you just reeled for a second, then lowered your leg, then lost;
I still don't feel right about this;
it wasn't the way to win a game;
a girl falling through the dark;
the sudden cold and wet;
the pull of something stronger than you can fight;
then the summer ending sadly;
my mother dragging me back to the city;
the public school like a prison;
the walls painted the sickest colors;
the lockers too, and those awful clocks;
and the metal detectors at the doors;
the security guards at the doors;
the cameras pointed at every kid in every room;
it was waking each morning to the darkest thoughts;
thoughts like this place will wreck you;
like the color of the walls will wreck you;
like these kids will fucking kill you;
my friends were at the private school;
my real friends with their ironed shirts and tightly pulled
back hair;
they would wait for me, my mother said;
they would not, I said;
they would forget, I said and, Fuck you, I said;
mornings, my mother walked me to school;
I didn't need her walking me;
but I was not to be trusted, she said;
at the front gate, she always tried to fix the way I looked;
she would touch my hair, and I never liked her touching me;
and the kids watching from the yard;

her hurt look when I ducked and ran;

her dumb hurt look that I still get sad to think;

there were science nights on the roof of the school;

telescopes pointed at planets;

some guy and I were forced by our mothers to go;

we would take our turns looking at the sky;

then we would sit on the other side of the roof;

we would smoke and look at the view;

there were as many lights there to look at;

as many things we couldn't explain;

one night, we got caught by the teacher;

the rumor was this teacher was a witch;

her nails were filed to absolute points;

we called her crazy to her face;

but all we got was yelled at then sent home;

and they called my mother, because of who I was;

and have I even told you who I was;

have I told you the kind of privileged I was;

before we lost our privilege, that is;

and my mother, can I say how furious;

needless to say I was going back to private school;

my punishment would be over;

everything would be back to what we called normal;

my short skirt, my blazer;

my hair pulled back in the tightest knot;

all of my friends there waiting for me;

all of them now so scared of me;

I was the real thing now coming to get them;

the ugly thing that would take them all the way down;

but was it my fault the girl fell in;

fault is too strong a word;

but did it happen because of me;

she was there for a second, then not;

then I stood for a second, stuck;

I mean I didn't at all help out;

and what was I thinking;

I wasn't thinking;

girls drowned falling from shorter heights;

they drowned in shallower water;

and I can't go back and do the right thing;

I can only tell you this girl was saved;

that the guys jumped in and saved her;

it had just been crazy for a while;

all this commotion on the jetty;

then all this commotion in the water;

then all this shit the following day;

the girl's mother, my mother, and someone had to be
punished;

for having a weak character;

for being addicted to being scared;

for being addicted to being watched;

and wasn't one terrible night enough;

wasn't one girl who drowned too much;

and what was I thinking;

and what was I feeling;

well, at least I still was feeling;

now, this is the definition of privilege;

this is the only one;

and guys on the jetty don't matter;

and nights on the jetty don't matter;

and nights on the jetty are nights on the dock;

and nights on the dock are nights of girls falling;

and all the girls falling is one girl drowning;

and that girl doesn't matter;

not by the end of summer;

not with that certain feeling;

that feeling one might call it a weight;

school around the corner;

months of snow and dark;

and the basketball game feels like a dream;

not a dream but a daydream of freezing time;

and if only I'd pressed pause;

made the planet's spinning stop;

just to think for a second;

or not think for a second:

but the girl was trying to block me;

she was trying to crowd me, and the guy said, Play nice;

so I said to the girl, Play nice;

then the girl had a decision to make;

be a good player or be a good girl;

so there came a moment the girl was distracted;

and I was standing alone in that moment;

and in that moment, the guy passed the ball;

I was close enough to shoot;

I admit, even shooting, I was still just trying to look good;

I shot the ball like look at me;

the guy clapped when I took the shot;

and the ball looked like it was going in;

and I wanted so bad for it to go in;

I wanted so much to score;

to walk away like no big thing;

to go back to the grass, like game over;

but the girl was in my face again;

I could feel my fingers breaking;

I fell to the ground for the longest time;

someone called time out;

then the guy was running toward me;

my hand was on top of his now;

and we'd been here before;

he'd saved me before;

but not like he saved the girl;

not like an actual savior;

jumping off of the jetty;

crashing into the water;

just to save some girl he never even liked;

I watched the rest from the sand;

I watched as the girl stumbled away, the guys holding on to her arms;

I waited there as the sky got light;

I sat there until my mother came to get me;

She could have drowned, she said;

I could have drowned, I said;

I should have drowned, I said;

and did I even mean it;

does it even matter;

either way, she looked so scared;

and she should have been scared;

we all should have been;

I don't need to explain this;

and eventually, this moment had to end;

it was time for us to go home;

and what else is there to say;

just the story, I guess;

the true story, I mean;

the terror I haven't told you;
so here, now, is the night on the dock;
so here is the girl who will drown;
here is the girl now on her knees;
and the kids who are going to push her;
the kids are too drunk, and the girl is too drunk;
and here is her just-fucked hair;
here is her perfect face;
here is the opening of her mouth;
and the words that aren't her words;
the words from something holy;
and the words from something not;
and the hands on her back, and the world goes dark;
then the thoughts that make me wild;
thunderstorms and fireflies;
sky and our sick fascination with stars;
the telescope on the roof of the school;
Jupiter's moons lined up like that;
or rings around Saturn like some kind of joke;
I could take you all the way into space;
I could take you so far back in time;
I could make you feel the things I feel;
or I could make this thing a fiction again;
say the basketball is going in;
say the dead are coming back;

Machines

There was the situation with his father's boots. It wasn't exactly a situation. It was just the size of his father's boots. And the way they stood at the foot of the bed. Like someone was standing in them.

The room looked like an old lady's room. There was a pilled white bedspread from another time. There were pillows from that other time. You could imagine an old lady dying in there. I mean in every way except for those giant boots.

I should say the boots were for fighting fires. That his father once fought fires at the shore. That he no longer did, but the boots still stood there in the room. And I should say I thought, so many times, walking past the room, to try them on.

At first, it was just for the joke. It was just to be like how dumb, me clomping around the house in those boots. But then I wondered what the boots would feel like. And what I would feel like in them. And then it was just this private thing, me and the boots at the foot of the bed, when the guy went out to get us beer.

On this night, the guy was at the market that I wouldn't go to with him. Because I sometimes went to the market too. And I wanted us to be a secret. And I liked waiting for him in his house. His father was never home at night. He was playing cards with guys. He was drinking with guys at a bar. So I played this game where I was the person who owned the house. It didn't involve anything more than walking around, touching the railing on the staircase. Pretending I was wearing a dress. Then I would sit alone in his father's room. His brother's room was next to his father's. Some nights, I could hear music. On this night, it was video games. It was things exploding and people screaming. And there were other sounds. Like animal sounds. Machines.

His brother was mostly a thing we ignored. In that way, in our commitment to this, this story isn't about him. But in another way, like the way in which his brother forced himself into my private scene, it is.

I should say in most ways my desires didn't feel right. Take the guy, for instance. He wasn't exactly a perfect fit. For the obvious reason, his being him, my being who I was. Take his father's boots, for instance. It didn't feel right my wanting to try them on. My wanting to clomp loudly through the house. But it wasn't some weird thing I had. It wasn't some replacement for something else. I had a father. I had my own boots.

I remember his father's last big fire. It was years before, and it was huge. The house on fire was also huge. The house on fire was on our side. Everyone was talking about it. How his father rushed into that burning house. He rushed through all those burning rooms. I remember his picture in the paper. I stared at that picture so hard my mother said, She's in love.

Back then, I didn't know this firefighter even had kids. And I wouldn't have cared, back then, besides. Back then, we didn't talk to the local kids. Back then, we didn't use the word *firefighter*. We used the word *fireman*. We used the word *policeman*. And *mailman*. Back then, I had a list of saviors, all of them guys. It was teachers and older guys at school. And older brothers of girls at school. If you'd told me, then, about the fireman's kid, I would have said fuck you. So if you'd told me, then, I would fuck that guy, some local guy.

I went with my father to the shore. It was winter, and it was time for him to get his things from the house. It was get them, my mother said, or she would destroy them. I didn't go to help my father get his things. I went because I wanted to see the shore. And my father didn't care who went.

At some point, the video game sounds stopped. It was like nothing was even out there then. It was like everything had been swallowed up, except this old-lady room and me in it. And I imagined I could go on like that forever. Just being in there like being, I imagined, on the moon.

I should say my desires, for many years, were all I had. Staring at a wall, thinking of a guy. Thinking about my future fame. Then, one day, I was done with this. Something bigger had taken over.

The last time I was with the guy, we were on the grass behind his house. He was on top of me and I felt like what I'll call dust. It's what I'll call dust floating up, floating down. When the storm came through, I could see the sky turn green around his face. The clouds I tried, first, to ignore. Then thunder like a sound of trees splitting. Like a thousand trees splitting all at once. And there was lightning now, and now there was rain. I wasn't scared of some storm coming down. I would have stayed there, under him, longer. But he pulled me to standing, and we ran like mad to the house.

No one ever stayed on our side in winter. There was snow on the ground and in the trees. There was no reason to be at the shore in snow. My father walked slowly though the rooms. He stared too long out of windows. He poured himself a drink and sat at the kitchen table. Eventually he would put his things into boxes. But first, he would sit there looking sad. I couldn't watch him be so weak. So I went for a ride. The snow in the trees looked blue. It looked better than it did in the city, where it first looked good, then piled for months and everyone complained.

I'm not going to delay what happened that night with the boots. I stood on the bed and climbed in. I'll tell you, it was challenging. I mean physically, and I mean in other ways. The boots were warmer than I thought they would be. They were higher too, and heavier. I couldn't even walk in them. So I was stuck at the foot of the bed. And I felt regret creeping in. I mean I knew, going in, there would be regret if I tried them on. But I also knew there would be regret if I didn't.

What I remember most about the fire is the two kids trapped in a room. This guy's father had rushed into the house to save them. But he wasn't able to save both kids. I mean he pulled both kids' bodies from the fire. But he could only save one of their lives.

And I remember, after, the house just stood there, half burned up, half not. They eventually took the whole thing down with what I imagine must have been big machines. This happened over the winter when no one was there to watch it. I mean the firefighter was there in winter. And his kids were there. But the people from our side were already forgetting that burned-up house and the kid who died and the entire shore how we did most years once we'd gone back to the city.

I stopped the car outside the guy's house. The house was different in the snow. You could almost call it charming. You could almost see smoke from a chimney. I sat in the car, the motor off. I felt like some kind of spy. It was quieter than it was in summer. Not silent though. There were sounds controlled by invisible things. All the different sounds of snow. The sounds of air and grass. In summer we'd left his front door open. We'd gone through his side door too. But now was different, and I couldn't just walk into his house. We'd already been back to school for months. We'd moved on in the ways one did from summer to winter. I was wearing a coat he'd never seen me in. And boots and socks pulled to my knees. I got out of the car. I walked to the door. I stood there and thought about knocking. I thought about breaking in.

My father put things into boxes that were our mother's things. There were pictures that were hers and there was clothing that was hers and there were kitchen tools and other things she would have wanted to keep. Later that night, when my father was sleeping, I took my mother's things out of the boxes. I took some of his things out too. I stored the things beneath my bed. And the following summer, back at the shore with my mother, I would put the things back in their places. And I would point out the things to my mother to see if and how she would actually destroy them.

It's hard to explain how I felt when I saw his brother in the doorway. First, I forced myself to laugh. But it didn't come out like laughing. It came out more like an animal sound, some fucked-up thing. His brother was just standing there, looking at me like I'd gone mad. I said, What the fuck are you looking at. I realize now he was the one who should have been asking questions. Like why are you in my father's room. And, why the fuck are you wearing my father's boots. Still, I stared him down so hard I could see him start to back away. Yes, I know he was young. And I know this makes me an asshole. But I was young then too. The world was young, I tell myself now. I mean no one had it figured out. We were all just things before other things. The star before the supernova. Hydrogen before the star.

The picture was of his father sitting on the curb. His face was dirty, and he seemed much younger than he was. I stared at that picture so much that day our mother said I was in love. And because I was in love, not with his father but with the picture of his father, I felt the shame I was meant to feel, and I ran to my room and slammed the door until things fell from the walls.

I suppose, looking back, there was more to the boots. That they had to mean something more. But standing there in them, I couldn't have known what it meant. Then I just thought I was being cute. Or being fun. Or getting revenge. Or getting saved. But on what, from what.

And I knew, even then, the guy would be gone very soon from my life. So what difference did any of it make. What difference, me standing in those boots. Me lying under him on the grass. I mean time would come in and change it all. The rides would shut down for the summer. The whole fucking shore would shut down. I would go back to school in the city. So what difference us rushing into the house. Me lying under him on his bed. His words at my ear. The sound of the storm.

I thought about breaking a window. I knew it was wrong to think this. Not to think it, but to break it. Even breaking a small window was wrong. Even the tiny window next to the door. There was nothing in the house I wanted to take. I just wanted, weird as it sounds, to reach inside.

Later, I thought of my footprints in the snow as evidence. And of threads falling from my coat. Hairs I could have shed. The entire system breaking down on the short path to his door.

And I thought of him walking through the snow, finding pieces of me and thinking they were pieces of someone else.

One night, my mother would take my father's remaining things to the terrace. She would lay his things on the terrace floor. She would cry, her hand in front of her face. Then she would smash his things with his other things until there was a pile of broken things. And she would leave the pile on the terrace. And the help would come in, eventually, to clean it.

His brother said, What are you doing. I said, What are you doing. I wasn't sure if this was funny now. Were we joking now. The guy would be back soon with beer. I felt like I had some decisions to make. About big things but also about right now. I said, I don't know what I'm doing. I said, Get me out of these fucking boots.

Then I fell straight back to his father's bed. I felt the boots slowly sliding off. Then I stood and felt weightless and his brother and I said nothing.

I often imagined being saved by a guy whose job it was to save. I often still imagine this. Ladders and nets and men in hats. Being carried through a smoke-filled room. Being carried like a child.

I often imagine being laid down on the ground. The grass wet beneath my back. Staring up at a hazy sky. A feeling like this is the end of something, the start of something else.

What I remember is how they talked after the fire. That I heard his father went mad. That he was stuck like that. Just stuck, my mother told me. Or my father told me. Or someone.

And then he was forgotten. Even I'd forgotten all this time. I mean I was so young when it happened. When he didn't save that kid. But looking into his room one night, I asked the guy about the boots. And it all came back. And I never told the guy I was once in love with a picture of his father.

His brother was going back to his video games. And did I want to play he said. I would for a second I said. So there I was sitting at his brother's desk. His room looked like a prison cell. I mean a cell in a prison for boys. He showed me one of his games. It turned out they weren't just violent. It turned out they were dirty too. Like you could undress some of the people. Like you could get them pretty much naked. And there were other things too. Like you could see people fucking. You could see a blowjob. You could see girl on girl. You wouldn't have found these things on your own. Someone had to show you these things. It involved going into secret rooms, looking around. His brother and I were laughing so hard. I said, I'm telling your father. He said, No you're not. And I would have kept playing, but the guy was back with the beer.

The guy's brother would OD. He would be on the wrong drug with the wrong kids and he would die. This would be many years later. This would be after he was a kid. It would be after a lot of things happened, and I would hear it from someone who heard it from someone else.

I don't know why I'm telling you this. Or why it broke me up so much to hear it. Or why I'm still so broken up. I mean I can barely remember his face. He was looking right at me, and I barely remember.

No, that's not even true. I do remember his face. The freckles across it. The space between his teeth. No, that's the face of the guy.

But I remember winning some video game. And lights blinking. A high five.

And I remember how, God, I almost rolled off the bed. I was so fucking stuck in those boots.

You can see this as a metaphor, if you want. How I wasn't good at getting out of things. How there are things I'm stuck in for good.

Like how I'm stuck in this body for good. Like how I'm stuck in this summer for good. How I'm stuck on a night and watching it all.

And it's guys staring into the water. Girls holding each other's arms. They're laughing into each other's hair. They're falling over laughing.

And I know how sound travels through water. Through plants and through fish. Through all of that trash.

So I know she can't hear them laughing. And I know they can't hear her scream.

Some nights, I sank too. Those nights, I sank like a stone. And I stayed at the bottom for as long as I could. I stayed there, waiting for something.

Don't make me tell you what it was.

I mean it doesn't matter now.

I mean nothing is going to save you.

And can you even save yourself.

Or are you stuck in it for good.

I mean I've been trying to tell just one story for nearly my entire life.

I mean I'm still trying to tell that same fucking story.

Still trying.

Acknowledgments

I wish to thank Chris Kamrath, Brittany Perham, Maria Barneson, Sebastian Currier, Lynne Layton, Stephen Hartman, Ryan Van Meter, Bruce Snider, Eileen Fung, Tom March, Tyler Mills, Lucy Corin, Michele Beck, Harold Meltzer, Lydia Conklin, James Hannaham, Carole Cebalo, Pauline Grant, Kelley Reese, Morgan Craig, Jonathan Santlofer, Lynn Callahan, Jeff Callahan, Sarah Dove, Gary Clark, David Grozinsky, Arista Alanis, Laurie MacFee, Peter Kline, Reese Kwon, Dave Madden, Randall Mann, Ayad Akhtar, Emily Kiernan, Bernadette Esposito, Gina Ruggeri, Normandy Sherwood, Michelle Seaton, Ani Tascian, Sarah Williams, Ian Jacoby, Emily Ballaine, Kate Liebman, Lucia Hierro, Carrie Mar, Katie Morton, Essie Chambers, Sergio de Regules, Andre Adler, and Horacio Camblong.

And special thanks to Steve Woodward, Ethan Nosowsky, Fiona McCrae, Marisa Atkinson, Katie Dublinski, Ethan Bassoff, Yaddo, the MacDowell Colony, the Civitella Ranieri Center, the Virginia Center for the Creative Arts, the James Merrill House, Vermont Studio Center, the Millay Colony, the American Academy in Rome, Jentel, the NYU Faculty Resource Network, and the University of San Francisco.

Susan Steinberg is the author of the story collections *Spectacle, Hydroplane,* and *The End of Free Love.* Her work has appeared in *McSweeney's, Conjunctions,* the *Gettysburg Review, American Short Fiction, Boulevard,* the *Massachusetts Review, Quarterly West,* and *Denver Quarterly.* She has been the recipient of a Pushcart Prize, a National Magazine Award, and a United States Artist Fellowship. She has held residencies at the MacDowell Colony, Yaddo, the Civitella Ranieri Center, the Virginia Center for the Creative Arts, the James Merrill House, the Millay Colony, Vermont Studio Center, the Wurlitzer Foundation, Jentel, Blue Mountain Center, and Ledig House. She earned a BFA in painting from the Maryland Institute College of Art and an MFA in English from the University of Massachusetts, Amherst. She teaches at the University of San Francisco.

The text of *Machine* is set in Adobe Garamond
Pro. Book design by Sarah Miner. Composition by
Bookmobile Design & Digital Publisher Services,
Minneapolis, Minnesota. Manufactured by Versa Press
on acid-free, 30 percent postconsumer wastepaper.